Dancing with Dan

D.E. BARTLEY

vinci
BOOKS

Vinci Books

vinci-books.com

Published by Vinci Books Ltd in 2026

1

A CIP catalogue record for this book is available from the British Library.
Paperback ISBN: 9781036733865
The EU GPSR authorised representative is Logos Europe, 9 rue Nicolas Poussion, 17000 La Rochelle, France contact@logoseurope.eu

By D.E. Bartley

Lakeside Ranch

Ladling with Luke

Dancing with Dan

O'Reilly Fight Club

Four Stepbrothers & I

Four Daddies & I

Faking it with the SEALs

Three Stepbrothers Save Christmas

Four Fiancés & I

Devil's Playground

Precious Little Rose

The Blood Moon Series

Rogue

Her Protector

To every girl who looked at a man in uniform and thought, "Yes, please!"
This one's for you.

Chapter One

LILY

"What's the matter? You look like you haven't slept in a month."

I turn to look at my new sister-in-law, Elli, and sigh.

"I feel like it. Every goddamn morning, Pops, Luke and Billy wake me up, talking outside of my window. I get they have to be up at the crack of dawn to work, but I don't!"

"Trust me, I get it; Luke is far from quiet in the mornings," Elli smiles sympathetically as she picks up her mug and frowns at it before taking a sip. "I miss real coffee as much as you are missing your sleep," she sighs, leaning back into her chair and placing a hand on her swollen belly.

At seven months pregnant, she looks ready to pop. Her bump is much bigger than Rachel's was in either of her pregnancies.

"No one can miss anything as much as you miss real coffee," I laugh, sitting at the kitchen table opposite her.

"Yeah, it might be my fault that Luke is waking you up. He's working more with each passing day. He says it's so he won't feel bad for not helping out as much when the baby arrives. But personally, I think he's avoiding spending time with my moody ass."

I laugh as she takes another sip of her drink, turns her nose up and places the cup back on the table.

"They could at least make this stuff taste like real coffee," she groans, pushing the mug away as if it offends her.

I absolutely love this woman. The best thing to come out of her and my brother's relationship is that I have the big sister I always wanted. Don't get me wrong; my other brother's wife, Rachel, is also a hoot, and I love her unconditionally. But with Elli, we have this connection and love of all the same things. She is also closer to my age, which I guess helps.

When she and Luke moved to the other side of the ranch four months ago, I couldn't have been happier to have them so close. I get to spend nearly every day with my favourite person. Even if she's now pregnant and can't come on any nights out, the fact she's close is enough.

"Legs? Why are you here and not resting back home?"

I turn to see Luke walking into the kitchen, closely followed by Pops and Billy. He heads straight to Elli and kisses her whilst placing a hand on her belly. The two of them will make the best parents to their tiny human when they're born.

"I told you I'd planned on coming over today to help Lil update her website," she replies, smiling, before it slips from her face. "Talking of Lil, you guys need to stop waking her up by being loud outside her window every morning!" she warns Luke before looking behind him to where Pops and Billy are both standing. They all instantly start protesting that they are quiet, but I roll my eyes whilst shaking my head.

"You are far from quiet, and you know it."

"Lily, if we were that loud, Grams would be complaining as well," Billy points out.

"Grams is nearly a hundred and as deaf as a fence post. She would sleep through the end of the world!" I shake my head again, knowing they won't listen.

I thought that with Rachel having Skyla and baby Imogen, I would no longer be seen as the baby of the family, and I would be taken seriously now and again, but I guess not.

"Thanks for trying, Elli. But we all know they won't pay a damn bit of notice to me or anything to do with me. Not until I finally move out anyway." I stand from my seat and walk over to place my mug in the kitchen sink.

"You are too young to move out, young lady, and you know it," Pops says, standing before me with his arms crossed.

"Luke was twenty when he moved out and went to university. Billy moved out at twenty-two; why am I any different?" I protest as I face my dad with my arms crossed over my chest.

"Because it was different with them. They can look after themselves."

"Why because they are male? Just because I was born female does not mean I'm incapable of living on my own or standing on my own two feet, Pops." I throw my hands up as I turn and walk out of the kitchen.

"Where are you going?" Pops calls after me.

"To get some more pictures for work! If that's okay with you? Or do I need a chaperone? Since I'm too weak and helpless to do anything alone."

I don't bother waiting for a reply or listening to whatever is being said in the kitchen. I grab my camera bag from the pegs at the front door and pull on my boots, not stopping until I am outside to tie them.

I drop to the porch floor and lace my walking boots, trying desperately to push away the irritation causing every muscle in my body to tense. I'm tired of being the baby and being treated differently from my brothers. So what if I'm a girl? It doesn't make me any different from them. I know Pops is just old-fashioned, it's his generation, and he doesn't mean anything by it, but it doesn't stop it from sucking, nevertheless.

"You know their heart is in the right place."

I turn to see Ma walking out of the front door behind me.

"You are his baby, and he worries about you; we all do," she says softly as she sits beside me on the porch.

"I'm not the baby anymore; he has grandkids now," I point out, which earns me a raised brow.

"But they aren't *his* babies. Not in the same way as you are," she reaches over and tucks some hair behind my ear.

Ma will always be the one to defend Pops and my brothers when they upset me; I know she's doing it to keep the peace, but sometimes I wish she would take my side, but she never does. The only one who ever seems to have my back is Elli, but even then, she doesn't like to cause arguments or for something to drive a wedge between her and Luke. They have only been married for a few months and are still very much in the honeymoon period.

I stand from my spot on the porch and pick up my camera bag. I need some space to calm down and recharge my tolerance levels.

"I gotta go. See you later, Ma." I turn my back to her and walk towards my car. Eager to place as much distance between myself and this house as possible. I hear Ma shouting for me to be careful, and I wave my hand in acknowledgement, not bothering to turn or reply.

I climb into the car and pull away from the house more aggressively than planned. The tyres skid momentarily on the gravel before getting traction and guiding me onto the ranch's driveway.

As I head to my favourite woods, I think about moving out of the ranch. If I did, I wouldn't need to answer to my family as much because right now, I have to tell them where I'm going and who I will be with. Even at twenty-two years of age, they treat me like a teenager.

Unlike my brothers, I've never been in any trouble with the law, and let's face it, they'd find out as the sheriff's deputy is Luke's best friend, who tells him everything that's been going on in town. Or there's the gossip tree that Ma is part of. I swear if someone sneezes in the wrong direction, the house phone rings with someone telling her about it.

I pull off our drive and onto the main road that passes several other ranches and leads to Mitchan Woods. By the time I reach my usual parking spot, I've decided that when I get home, I will start looking into the housing market and find somewhere to buy or rent. I need to be independent, which won't happen while I live under my parent's roof.

Chapter Two

DAN

I walk out into the mild afternoon sun and shield my eyes from the glare coming off the police cruiser in front of me.

"Keep your door closed and locked, ma'am, and I'm sure you will have no more problems," I say, turning to look at old Mrs Hall.

"I have lived in this house all my life, and I ain't ever had to lock my door before," she argues. I roll my eyes as I turn my back to her and head towards the car.

"Things change, Mrs Hall. This old town isn't as it used to be. You have a good day now, and call if you have any more problems," I add before climbing into the car, where Sheriff Hobbs is grinning at me like the child he is.

"You fucking prick."

Sheriff Hobbs roars, laughing as I pull my seatbelt around myself.

"Mrs Hall was robbed, Deputy Thomas. It's your duty to protect our community and investigate the crime," he states, trying desperately to keep a straight face.

"She left her back door wide open, and an animal got in

and ate the sausages she left out on the counter. That's not a crime, it's stupidity!"

Sheriff Hobbs roars, laughing again as he drives us slowly through town. He starts listing the things we need to get sorted out, but I'm not paying attention. I'm nodding and humming in the right places, but inside I'm screaming for him to shut up and let me out of this goddamn car.

We pull up outside of the station and climb out with the Sheriff still talking away about fuck knows what.

"I'm fixin' for a salad. I'll be right back," I call, jogging away from him and the station. I hear him shouting for me to pick up his usual. I hold up my thumb without turning to check he can see me.

As soon as I'm out of view, I tone the jog down to a slow walk and shove my hands into my trouser pockets.

What the hell am I doing with my life? Being a police officer is all I've ever wanted to do. But, nothing exciting ever happens in this small town. I know all officers feel like this eventually, which is why the retirement age is relatively young compared to other forces in the US or even just here in Alabama. But in our town, the biggest crime is the occasional bar brawl, a drunk and disorderly, or even an animal stealing sausages from an open window or kitchen door. Where's the excitement in that?

I've been feeling more and more trapped recently like nothing is ever going to change in my life. It could be because I've watched my best friend, Luke, fall in love, get married, and now have a baby on the way in the short space of twelve months. It could also be because I can't seem to meet anyone who keeps me interested for more than a few days. I've dated or slept with near enough every woman in this tiny town, and I still haven't met anyone I want to share things with, like late-night rides or drinks in town with friends. Maybe I've been a player for so long that I don't recognise a catch when I see one, or I've already missed my chance of happiness.

I stop outside the local café where we all get our lunches and let out a sigh before walking inside.

"Howdy, Dan!"

I turn to see my other best friend, Mitch, sitting at a table with his father. They work together, building barns and sheds for those in the community. They enjoy working together, and neither complain about anything other than the weather when it stops them from working. What I wouldn't give to enjoy my work as much as they do.

"Hey. How's it going?" I ask, heading over to the table and taking a seat. Mitch, Luke, and I have been best friends for as long as I can remember. Our families see each other as family, and we never have to worry about interrupting family time.

"Not much, just about to head over yonder to Johnson's place. His boys need a hand with a shed, and their pops isn't up for it like he used to be. He's starting to feel his age," Mitch's old man, Doug, chuckles as he drinks his mug of tea.

"You're both as old as dirt, old man, so pack it in," Mitch sighs, shaking his head at his father, who laughs at him before turning his attention to me. "You still hosting the game tonight? Need me to bring anything along?" Mitch asks.

"Nah, I have everything in. What time you coming over?"

"About seven?" Mitch asks.

"Yeah, sounds good to me. I'll let Andy know and see if he can make it," I reply, pulling my phone out of my pocket.

"I'll give Luke and Billy a heads up when I get to their place"

I nod as I read a message from a girl I saw last week. I roll my eyes as she asks what I'm up to and if I want to meet up. Isn't the fact that I haven't made contact with her in a week not enough of a sign that I'm not interested? She was loud and seriously thought too much of herself. She screamed high maintenance, which I'm not into.

Under the message, I see one I have been waiting for. As I read it, my stomach tightens with anticipation.

"Earth to Dan, you listening?"

I look back to Mitch and see him frowning at me.

"Sorry, what?"

"I said, who has pissed you off? You've been tense since you walked through the door."

I sigh, rub my tired face, and close my phone quickly, hoping he doesn't see the message.

"Just been a crap day. I got to go; Sheriff will wonder where his sub is." I stand up and say a quick "See ya later" to Doug and Mitch before heading over to the counter and ordering our food.

I can feel Mitch's eyes on me the whole time I'm there. He knows me better than anyone, even Luke, and will know something's going on. But how do I tell my best friend that I've been looking into moving out of state, and it may be happening sooner than I thought?

Chapter Three

LILY

I'm so glad I came out today. The fresh winter air and the crunch of the leaves under my feet is just what I needed to clear my mind.

Now that I've calmed down, I realise I may have blown the whole situation out of proportion back home. I know Pops and my brothers don't mean any harm in how protective they are, but I feel smothered. I know it's time that I moved out and started living my life the way I want and not how others expect me to.

I have plenty of money coming in, so I can afford it. Thanks to Elli and all the work she has put into my website and helping me advertise, my photography sells worldwide, and I can't get the prints out quickly enough.

When I told my family I wanted to turn my hobby into a business, they were all encouraging and supportive, but I don't think they expected me to succeed. To be honest, I didn't expect to have the success that I did. In fact, I thought I would have to work a second job on top of this to make ends meet. Instead, I'm making four figures a month easily and even on a bad month, I never drop more than a couple of grand. That's more than enough for me to move out and live comfortably. Worse case I could see if any of my friends want to move in with me and share the bills. Anything has to be better than still living at home when you are nearly twenty-three years old.

I stop in my tracks as I spot a doe a short distance from me. I squat down as slowly and quietly as possible whilst lifting my camera to snap a picture. Just as I'm about to take one, a tiny fawn bounds into view and stands next to their mother. It's rare for a fawn to be born this late in the year, but it does happen. I know I can't miss the opportunity to photograph a fawn with the winter foliage around it. A picture like this could sell well.

I watch through my camera lens as the mother feeds and tries to keep the fawn under control. She is fighting a losing battle as this one seems to be full of beans and unable to stay still for longer than a few seconds at a time.

I follow them from a distance for about half an hour, unable to resist the cuteness of the fawn as it leaps around its mother and begs for attention. I have more than enough pictures to work with, but I can't seem to stop. I love nothing more than watching wildlife as it goes about its day, none the wiser that they are being watched. These two creatures in front of me are beautiful and mesmerising.

Just as I snap a picture of the doe reaching up to pull some foliage from a bush, something catches her attention and mine. I watch her ears start moving around, and she looks towards her right as if expecting danger. The fawn picks up on this and quickly moves to her side, and they also start looking around, mimicking their mother's behaviour. I look to the side of them and spot it: a cougar hiding in the bushes. It's so fixated on its prey that it hasn't noticed me.

Luckily, Pops taught me from a young age never to go anywhere without a whistle to blow if I got into trouble or saw a creature I wanted to scare away. I lift the whistle to my lips and start blowing hard whilst jumping out of my hiding spot. I know it's a risky move; the cougar could attack me, but all I can think about is protecting the mother and her baby.

All three animals jump as the whistle blows for the first time. For a fleeting second, they turn to look at me, and I don't wait to blow it a second time, which successfully scares them away from me and each other.

I keep blowing the whistle repeatedly to ensure all creatures have left and are a good distance from me. The last thing I need right now is the cougar circling back around and coming after me. I don't want to be its replacement meal, thank you very much.

"Hello? Is anyone hurt out here?"

I spin around to where the voice is coming from the left of me. I stop blowing the whistle as they call out again, checking if I'm okay. I take a few steps towards the voice when a young man comes into view.

"Are you okay, ma'am? I heard your whistle."

"Yeah, sorry, I saw a cougar," I explain, waving the whistle at him. His jaw drops, and he starts looking around frantically.

"A cougar? Where?" He looks ready to run, and I can't help laughing.

"It's gone that way; I scared it off. You're safe, for now at least," I tease as I stop in front of him, and he visibly relaxes. "Lily Johnson," I announce, holding out my hand. He takes it in a firm grip and shakes.

"Tim Gerald."

"So what brings you out here, Tim?" I ask as I admire

his suit and tie. You don't look like you're hiking, that's for sure."

He looks down at his outfit and laughs.

"No, I'm taking pictures of a property my dad is trying to sell," he explains, rubbing his neck.

"Oh, you're Mr Geralds's son! The estate agent in town," I exclaim. What are the odds that I'm considering buying a place to live, and an estate agent walks right into my path?

"There's a cabin for sale around here?" I ask excitedly. Tim nods with a smile on his face.

"Would you like to see it?" he asks, holding out his hand and showing me the way. I quickly let him lead me out of the trees and towards a log cabin surrounded by nothing but trees, with a dirt road leading away from the property.

I couldn't even guess how many times I've been in these woods over the years. They've always been my favourite place to come when the guys were picking on me, or Ma and Pops were getting on my nerves, but not once have I ever seen this place. Sure, the woods are vast compared to the others around here, but to miss the cabin entirely is madness.

Tim starts telling me about the property as he leads me inside, and I look around.

The place is beautiful and rustic. Even with the thick dust that coats every surface, it looks perfect for me. There are two bedrooms, a large sitting room, and an open log fire surrounded by a beautifully carved fireplace. My brother Luke may be able to build just about anything with wood, and his carvings are always breathtaking. But there is something about this fireplace that even he couldn't achieve.

I walk up the wooden staircase towards the two rooms and bathroom. Again, everything is covered in thick dust and needs a good airing. The musty smell in the air would soon disappear if the windows were left open for a bit and the place had a good clean.

"How long has it been empty?" I ask as I look at the built-in wardrobe in the main bedroom. There is also a king-size wooden bed. I dread to think what lives in its mattress now; it would no doubt need a new one.

"Approximately three years. The structure itself is sound and needs very little work done to it, but the furniture inside and the plumbing may need to be torn out at new put in," Tim explains as he runs his finger over the top of a chest of drawers, leaving a long void in the thick dust.

"How much is it selling for?" I ask, looking out the window at the view of the forest surrounding the cabin.

"Why? You thinking of buying?" I can hear the disbelief in Tim's voice.

"Funny enough, I was going to come down and speak to your Pops later about any property he had for sale." I look around the main bedroom and can see myself at home here. "This would be perfect," I add with a smile.

Tim watches me for a moment before a big smile appears on his face, and he stands to attention.

"Tell you what, let me be the one to sell it to you, and we can come to an affordable deal." He steps forward and holds his hand out for me. "I promise I will look after you," he smiles. I take his hand excitedly and shake it.

"Deal."

Chapter Four

LILY

A few hours later, I take a deep breath before walking into the house. I can hear from outside that the whole family is here, and I can't decide whether that's a good thing or not.

"Aunty Lily!" I only just catch an excited Skyla as she launches herself at me as soon as I enter the dining room.

"Howdy, Skyla. How was school?" I ask as I place her back on her feet. She may only be six, but she is too big for me to carry these days. I don't have the strongest arms, which is why I'm no good about the ranch. Even docile Mitzy, Elli's horse, can pull me if she wants something out of her reach.

"It was boring. They only let us paint for ten minutes. Instead, I had to do math," she declares as she screws up her face in distaste. I copy her, which earns me a smile.

"Only weirdos like math," I tell her.

"Uncle Luke likes maths, and you can't get much weirder than him," Elli laughs as she walks into the room carrying two plates. Okay, walk may be the wrong word; waddling may be more accurate for what she's doing.

"Legs, I told you not to carry anything," Luke declares, jumping to his feet to take the plates from her. Elli moves them out of his way and proceeds to place them on the table.

"Cowboy, I swear to God, I'm going to snap if you don't stop fussing over me like an old mother hen!" she warns with her hands on her hips. "If Rachel can carry Skyla whilst pregnant, I sure as hell can carry a couple of plates. Now sit down and shut up!" She points to his place with such force I have to bite my lip from laughing out loud when he does as he's told.

"By the way, it's math, not maths. You ain't in England now; there's no 's'at the end." Luke ducks quickly and scrambles out of Elli's reach as she goes to slap him around the back of the head. The rest of us roar, laughing as Luke laughs and pulls a pouting Elli towards him, making sure to keep her arms by her side as he kisses her.

"You are lucky there are children present, Cowboy," Elli warns, fighting back a smile. Luke leans in and kisses her again before letting her go.

"Right, stop winding up the pregnant lady. Sit down and eat," Ma announces as she walks into the room with two more serving dishes. Everyone quickly takes their seats around the table.

I say a quick 'hi' to Rachel as I sit beside her and press a kiss to Imogen's head as she feeds from her mother's breast. She is such a beautiful and content baby, the complete opposite of Skyla when she was born. Since the moment she found her voice, Skyla has made sure she always has everyone's attention. We were a little worried about how she would be when the baby was born, but she loves her sister more than anything in the world. She tells her stories, helps Rachel change her diapers, and gets her anything she needs.

"You alright, Lily?"

I turn to see Pops sitting at the head of the table next to me. He reaches over and places a hand over mine on the table.

"About what I said before," he starts, but I place my other hand over his and give him a smile.

"It's fine, Pops. There's no need for apologies," I reply. He nods once, and I release his hand so he can start piling the food on his plate.

I look around the table and start to dish up my own food. I love Ma's cooking, especially when she has made my favourites: fried chicken, mashed potatoes, and gravy. I place it on my plate, and soon, we all start digging in and chatting among ourselves. I make it halfway through my food before Elli gets my attention.

"Did you manage to get any good shots today, Lil?"

I look up from my plate to see her smiling at me. Nerves start to knot in my stomach as I nod slowly.

"Yeah, I saw a deer with a fawn," I explain. After a few minutes of the others asking about how old I thought the fawn was and wondering why it was born so late, Pops pipes in with another question.

"What else did you do today? You were out for a long time."

I chew on the inside of my cheek and take a deep breath.

"Well, I kinda bought a house."

I hear people's cutlery hitting their plates as Pop's mouth drops open.

"What do you mean you *kinda* bought a house?" Billy asks as I try to appear calmer than I'm feeling.

"Okay, I bought a house. A cabin in Michan Woods, to be precise. It's been empty for a few years and is a bit of a fixer-upper, but I fell in love with it as soon as I saw it and knew I had to own it."

Pop looks up at Ma, who is staring at me.

"Annie, have a word with your daughter," Pop warns as he points his fork at me.

"I don't need a word. I'm able to make my own decisions," I snap as I look at Pops.

"Lily, how did you afford to buy a house? Where will you get the money for the mortgage, repairs, furniture, and so on? I know you think you can afford this, but - "

I snap my attention to my mom, who's looking a little shell-shocked.

"I have plenty of money to do all of that. The cabin was a steal, and even Mr Gerald said it was a bargain. He's already put me in touch with a few people to help with the repairs, and they are coming out tomorrow to give me quotes."

"Nope, not happening. You are not moving out."

I turn my attention back to Pops, whose jaw is clenched as he shakes his head.

"You can't stop me from moving out," I point out, trying desperately to keep calm.

"Oh, just watch me, young lady. While you live under my roof, you will do as I say," Pop snaps, taking me by surprise. He never snaps at me, not like this anyway.

"That's the point, Pops. I won't be living under your roof," I say, standing from the table and looking around at my family. The girls all look like they don't know what to say or do, and the guys are tense.

"Lily, you are not moving into a cabin in the middle of nowhere. It's not safe," Luke starts, throwing his napkin onto his plate.

"Luke's right, I won't let you put yourself in danger like this," Billy adds as he pushes his chair back from the table.

"Oh, come on. You," I snap, pointing at Billy, "moved out when you were twenty-one. And you," I turn my attention to Luke, "went to university when you were twenty. What is the difference between you two and me?" I yell.

"Oh, don't start all this again. This has nothing to do with you being a girl. It's about you living in a cabin in the middle of nowhere!" Billy yells, causing Imogen to scream and Skyla to cry. Rachel stands from the table and looks at her husband.

"Stay and discuss this like adults. I will take the kids out." She starts to lead the kids from the room. But before leaving, she turns and looks at me.

"I will always have your back, but I agree with your brother. The cabin doesn't sound safe. If you want to move out, I will help you find a place myself, but please reconsider."

I watch as she leaves the room with the two crying kids.

"Now look what you've done. You upset the kids," Billy starts, but I turn to face him with a look that makes him stop in his tracks.

"You upset the kids. You were the one shouting like an idiot. God, you are all being so unreasonable." I turn to walk out of the door and hear Elli calling my name.

"Lily, stop, please. You know they are just worried about you. Come back and talk about this."

I turn around and see her standing up, leaning on the table.

"There's nothing to talk about. I'm moving out as soon as the cabin is ready. I'll leave sooner if you don't stop trying to control me and everything in my life!" I hear their raised voices as I walk from the room and up to my room.

I don't know why I thought they might actually support me in this. Let's face it: they will always see me as the baby of the family, no matter how old I am.

Chapter Five

DAN

"And she thinks she's going to be just fine and dandy living out there in the middle of bumfuck nowhere. I bet she can't even get a phone signal out there!"

I look to Luke, who's been in a foul mood since he arrived. Billy hasn't been much better, but as always, Luke is the one ranting and raving, and Billy nods in agreement.

"I'm sure she has thought about all of that, Luke. Lily isn't stupid."

From the way the Johnson brothers glare at me, I know I've said the wrong thing.

"How would you feel if it was your kid sister? I bet you would be just as concerned," Billy points out as he shuffles the cards.

"The difference is my kid sister, and yours are two completely different people. My sister was knocked up by the time she was sixteen. Your sister studied hard and worked even harder to make a name for herself. Lily is level-headed, Sharon is not."

Billy mutters something under his breath as he starts dealing out the cards. I look to Mitch who is looking at us around the table, keeping his head down, whilst drinking my good bourbon. Nothing new there, then.

"Look, I get you are both annoyed as hell, shit, I get it. But moaning about it isn't going to change her mind. The paperwork's been signed, and she has the keys. There is nothing you can do about it." I pick up my cards and curse silently at my rubbish hand.

"Maybe," Luke mutters as he looks at his own cards.

"What do you know about the place? Any idea why it's been empty for years?" Billy asks. I shake my head whilst picking up my drink.

"Nothing about it rings a bell, but I'll have to ask about it at work."

"Well, if it's bad, you need to tell us. It might be enough to put her off moving in there," Luke says, sipping his drink.

"I'll see what I can find, but I'm not making any promises." I watch the two brothers nod in agreement. "Great, now can we please play a few rounds of cards before one of you gets called away by your ball and chains," I tease as Mitch laughs out loud. We love giving them both shit for being married. We know we can get away with it as their wives are great and like to wind them up as much as we do. The two brothers mutter something in agreement, and the game finally starts to unfold as their mood starts to lift.

It doesn't take long, and the conversation drifts to Billy's kids and Luke's baby on the way. The more they talk about them, the more jealous I become. I want what they have, and I'm once again reminded that I won't get that here, not in this town or maybe even this state.

It's half passed ten, and the brothers have left to get home to their families, leaving Mitch, me, and a bottle of bourbon. As usual, Mitch has drunk far too much to even think of attempting the short walk home so will crash in my spare room.

"You've been quiet tonight."

I turn to look at Mitch and find him watching me.

"I've not had much to add to the conversation," I answer, sipping my drink. I can feel Mitch still watching me and sigh as I look back to the sofa he is lying on. "What?"

"It was more than that. What are you hiding?"

"Nothing." I know I answer too quickly, and he picks up on it.

"How long have we been friends?" he asks, sitting up and placing his glass on the coffee table in front of him.

"Too fucking long," I sigh, downing the rest of my drink as I gear myself up for the long lecture I'm about to get.

"You are my brother, and I know when something's wrong. I saw how you looked at your phone in the café earlier, so spill it. What's going on?" Mitch is giving me his full attention, and I know I have no choice but to come clean.

"Fine, I'm sick of the job and regret becoming a police officer. Nothing ever happens around here, and I'm tired of the same old callouts. I feel more like animal control than I do an officer of the law." I wait for Mitch to say he told me so. He always said I was living a fool's dream when I went into the police. He thought I should learn a trade like him and that I would regret not listening to him. He never said anything again. Mitch isn't like that; he will sit on something, and when you prove him right, he will remind you he knows us better than we know ourselves and move on.

"You don't regret it, not deep down."

I stare at him for a moment before frowning.

"What? No big *I told you so*?"

Mitch shakes his head and runs his fingers through his hair.

"No, because I was wrong back then."

"Can I have that in writing?" I ask, amazed. He rolls his eyes and sits back on the sofa before putting his feet up on the coffee table and relaxing.

"You love your job, and you make a damn good cop. I might have had my doubts when you first said you wanted to be an officer, but you proved me wrong." He places an arm over the back of the sofa and relaxes a little further. "What you don't like is that it's not the fast life you imagined. You thought it would get you every girl in town, and for a while, it did. But now you want more and are worried you can't get it. The job is something you can control, so you choose to focus on that and want to change it when what you really need to do is stop sleeping around and settle down."

Damn, that's deep for him and also spot on, but I'm not going to admit that to him, and he knows it.

"Fine, don't accept that's the truth. But I saw the way you looked when the guys were talking about their kids. You want that, and there's no hiding it." Mitch pushes himself up from the sofa and stretches. "I'm going to crash; I have to be out of here by seven. Thanks for hosting the game and the drink. It's my turn next." He walks towards the lounge door before calling out, "Think about what I said, Dan. Ideally, before you end up old and alone because you have fucked every woman in town who will give you the time of day."

As Mitch disappears out of view, I sigh and sit back in

my chair, wishing I still had some drink left in my glass. I know he's right, and I know I need to change something before I drive myself mad, which is why I've been putting things into place and will tell him when I am good and ready, whenever that may be.

Chapter Six

LILY

I look around at the lounge and still can't believe it's mine. Everything in here belongs to me, and I couldn't be happier.

It's been a week since I first saw the property, and the excitement hasn't worn off. In fact, I would say I'm happier than I was that first day.

"Hey, Lil, are you in here?"

I turn to see Tim standing at the door with a smile on his face. He is dressed in his usual suit, shirt and tie.

"Hey! What are you doing here?" I ask as I head to the door and give him a hug.

Tim has been a fantastic help over the last week. He found me a plumber and electrician who both gave me affordable quotes. He's also been a great friend when I have needed one. My family is still giving me a hard time about this place, but Tim has listened as I moaned and gave me advice when I needed it.

"I thought I would pop around and see how the renovations were coming along." He looks around at the lounge where I have been giving it a fresh coat of paint. "It's looking so good in here; do you need a hand?" he asks, walking further into the room.

"You're in your suit," I point out, laughing. Tim looks down at his clothes and smiles.

"That's easily amended." He shrugs off his jacket and loses his tie. As he starts rolling up his shirt sleeves, I notice he has a full sleeve of tattoos on his right arm. He is also very well-built and obviously works out regularly.

"Like what you see?"

I look at Tim's face and smile.

"Sick tat."

He looks down at the tattoo and grins.

"Yeah, I love it. Pa makes me cover it when I'm at work. He says it's off-putting to the clients." He holds out his arm to give me a better look. I take his arm and start moving it around so I can see all the details.

"It's very cool. I love that flower; it's so pretty," I smile, pointing to a pink and white flower that twists and wraps its way up his arm.

"Not as pretty as you."

I slowly look up to find Tim smiling at me fondly. Shit.

"Uh, thanks." I let go of his arm and step back nervously. I see his smile falter slightly, making me feel guilty. "That's nice of you to say," I add, forcing a smile, hoping he thinks I'm just embarrassed and not uncomfortable. Tim smiles and takes a step forward.

"Lily, I was wondering - "

"Knock, knock! Anybody in here?"

I look to the door to see my brother's best friend, Dan, in his uniform smiling at me.

"What are you doing here?" I ask, rushing towards him, glad to put some distance between Tim and me. I throw my arms around Dan's neck, taking him by surprise. "Thank God you're here," I whisper into his ear as I let him go and hold his arm.

"Dan, this is Tim, who helped me buy the cabin," I announce, clinging to his arm. "Tim, this is Deputy Daniel Thomas," I add. Tim steps forward with his hand out.

"Of course, I know, Deputy Thomas. It's good to see you, sir."

Dan nods and shakes his hand.

"You're Tim Gerald, right? How's your father after the break in the other week?" Dan asks, causing Tim's smile to falter for half a second.

"He's fine. Luckily, very little was taken."

"You had a break-in? You never mentioned that."

Tim looks at me and smiles.

"Nothing to tell. Some morons came in and stole some petty cash. Luckily, Pa had cashed up that night, which he doesn't usually do." I can hear the frustration in his voice, and I have a feeling he is still pissed with whoever broke into his dad's place.

"Anyway, I didn't know you two knew each other," Tim points out, looking between Dan and me. I freeze for a second, wondering if Dan will let slip we aren't close, but instead, he places a hand over mine, resting on his arm and smiles down at me.

"We go way back, don't we, Lily bear?" the bastard smirks, using the stupid nickname he gave me when I was six. He knows I hate it, and there's nothing I can do about it.

"Sure do, Daniel," I reply, knowing he hates being called his full name as much as I do Lily bear.

"Well, I hope I didn't interrupt anything when I walked

in?" Dan asks, turning his attention to Tim, who steps back while shaking his head.

"No sir, I was just going to help Lily with some painting, but." Tim lifts his wrist and looks at his watch. I hear Dan snigger slightly and quickly try to cover it with a cough. I nudge him with my elbow whilst giving him a warning look. "Oh, I forgot I have a meeting in half an hour with Pa and a potential client, so I had better be off," Tim continues whilst grabbing his things and heading for the door.

"Thanks for popping around, Tim, and for all your help," I call out. He waves as he rushes out of the door.

"Take care, and shout if you need anything else done for the place," he calls back as he reaches his car.

"Thanks for all you've done for my Lily. I'll make sure to tell your father what a great job you're doing when I see him next," Dan calls out as he pulls his arm from me and wraps it around my shoulder.

"You are loving this," I growl through gritted teeth to ensure I still have a smile on my face.

"Every second," Dan replies, laughing. Tim pulls away too quickly, kicking gravel up from the makeshift road as he goes. As soon as he's out of sight, I shrug off Dan's arm as he laughs aloud.

"Aww, I think you hurt his feelings," he teases as he follows me into the cabin.

"I never thought I would be so glad to see you, jackass," I sigh as I fall onto the couch, which throws up a load of dust, causing me to cough.

"Nice place," Dan chuckles over the sound of my hoarse coughs.

"If you came here to wind me up, just leave," I snap before looking at him properly. "Why are you here? Did Luke send you?" I ask, crossing my arms over my chest. I watch Dan look around for somewhere to sit before wiping down a stool I've used to stand on when painting.

"Actually, Mrs Guest, who is your closest neighbour, by the way, has been noticing someone hanging around in the woods. She wanted me to check it out, and I thought I would give you a heads-up as well."

I guess that makes sense. Mrs Guest lives just over half a mile away, so whoever she saw could have headed this way.

"Thanks, I'll keep an eye out," I answer, standing from my seat.

"The place is nice. I can see why you like it. It's peaceful and quiet."

I look at Dan and frown.

"But?" I ask, waiting for him to agree with Luke.

"But nothing," he replies, standing from his seat and walking forward. "I get it, Lils; your family smoother you. They may only do it because they care, but they have to let you make your own decisions at some point. Let's face it, you're a damn sight smarter than my Sharon. As much as I love my nephew, and she is a fantastic mama, I do wish she had experienced more of life before having a baby."

"I wish you would tell my brothers that," I sigh, looking around at my lounge. I had hoped they would help me get it ready to live in. I wanted them to put the Johnson mark on the place—not because it would be done for free, but because it would be them.

"I have, and it didn't go down well. But I will keep trying, okay?"

I look at Dan and nod.

"Thank you, Daniel," I grin playfully.

Dan rolls his eyes and turns away from me.

"You're welcome, Lily bear," he calls as he walks towards the door. He stops as he goes to exit and turns back to look at me. “If you need anything and don’t want to call your family, call me.” He turns back around and pulls his business card from his wallet. “Any time, day or night, you ring me.”

“I will. Thanks again, Dan,” I say, taking the card.

“Any time, Lils. Be careful out here, okay? Keep your doors locked until I determine if this guy is dangerous to others.”

I nod, not knowing what else to say.

Dan smiles and walks out of the cabin and towards the police cruiser.

“See you later, and try not to get eaten out here. The paperwork’s a bastard for animal killings!” he yells as he climbs into the police car.

“Whatever!” I call back, laughing. I can see Dan grinning as he pulls away and heads down towards the road leading to town.

Walking back into the cabin, I close the door, look at it briefly, and quickly lock it. Even if my family think otherwise, I’m not an idiot. Dan said to be careful, and so I am.

I look around the lounge and sigh at the amount of work left to do. I might as well crack on and see how much I can get done before returning to the ranch. I pick up the paintbrush, hit play on my MP3 speakers, and start to paint as Taylor Swift’s voice fills the room.

Chapter Seven

LILY

I look around my childhood bedroom and wonder if I'm doing the right thing.

I love the little home I've created for myself out there in the woods. Don't get me wrong, I don't regret buying it at all. However, there's still work to be done on the place, but the tension at the ranch is becoming too much. Pops is hardly speaking to me; the guys keep telling me I'm causing too much stress on our parents and that I need to stop being so selfish. Elli and Luke even had a blazing row in the kitchen the other day, and Luke blamed me. It's all gotten out of hand, and I need to get out of here.

I always pictured moving out as a big, happy event, one I would look back on fondly. Instead, I'm hurting my family and causing them a load of heartache. But I know if I back down on this, they will keep trying to control my life, and I can't do it anymore.

I pick up my stuffed bear from the bed and place him carefully in my suitcase. I had hoped my last night in my family home would be a joyous occasion, but instead, I will be upstairs in my room, just waiting for morning so I can go.

A knock comes from my bedroom door, and I let out a sign.

"What do you want, Luke?"

The door opens, and he stands in the doorway, looking around my nearly empty room.

"So, tomorrow's the big day, huh?" he asks, leaning against the doorframe with his arms crossed over his chest.

"Yep. You here to tell me what a mistake I'm making again?" I ask sarcastically. Luke sighs and shakes his head.

"No, I'm sick of the arguing, as is everyone else." Luke pushes himself away from the door frame and heads over to the bed; he sits beside me and picks up one of my teddies.

"I spoke to Dan today. He said he popped by your place the other day."

I nod and wait to see if he knows about the guy Mrs Guest is convinced is stalking her. I know Luke will use it as proof I shouldn't be moved out there on my own if he has.

"He said it's a nice quiet place, and he only gets called out to animals causing damage. There is never anything that would put you in danger."

I make a mental note to thank Dan. It would have been easy for him to tell Luke all about the guy seen walking around or even how uncomfortable Tim made me.

"I guess we all need to just accept this is happening and support you."

"And hope it all goes wrong so you can gloat and point out you told me so?" I sigh. I'm too tired to beat around the bush tonight.

"No."

I turn to look at Luke, frowning, to find him looking back at me.

"You are my baby sister, Lil; there is nothing I wouldn't do for you. But I also need to accept you are growing up, and you have always been sensible and older than your years. Maybe it's time to accept you're probably more grown up than me some of the time."

"Only some?" I ask, smirking at him. He nudges me with his shoulder, and I laugh, nudging him back.

"Fine, most of the time. You happy now?"

"Yep."

He rolls his eyes as he stands and places the bear in my open suitcase.

"Whatever. Now come on, I'm starving, and Ma's made your favourite," Luke says, heading towards the door.

"You're staying for dinner?" I ask, jumping to my feet.

"We all are. Billy, Rach and the kids are downstairs, too," Luke says as he looks towards me. I freeze as my good mood slips. "No one is going to ruin tonight for you. We've all had enough of the bickering and want to see you happy. Even if that means away from the rest of us."

I jump forward and wrap my arms around his neck. Luke chuckles as he hugs me back.

"Thank you," I whisper, swallowing back the tears.

"Don't thank me yet. Elli made the pudding, and we all know there's a chance it's not edible," he jokes as I step back, smiling. "Now, come on; otherwise, you know Billy's going to eat all the chicken." Luke throws his arm around my shoulders and smiles as we walk to the top of the stairs and head down to the dining room, where I can hear my whole family talking and laughing together, as it should be.

It's ten PM when I finally head to my room.

It turned out to be a great night, and everyone seemed a lot more supportive than they had been since I announced that I'd brought the cabin.

Billy, Luke, and Pops are going to help me move tomorrow. They'll also see if they can help with anything around the cabin. Billy even offered to check the roofing for me, and Luke the fireplace. Things are finally looking up, and I realise I have a lot to thank Dan for. Luke and Billy told me tonight how Dan said they needed to give me a break and that I was in as much danger here on the ranch as I am out there.

I pull out my phone and open it to message him. After Dan gave me his number, I saved it in my phone for emergencies. I would be stupid not to take him up on his offer. He is an officer of the law, after all. How many people can say they have a deputy's direct number? It certainly makes me feel safer knowing he is only a call away. I type out about three different messages before sending one.

Lily: Hi, I just wanted to say thank you for speaking to my brothers. It really helped, and they seem to have finally accepted that I am moving out.

Short and sweet, straight to the point. I don't see the point in beating around the bush with Dan; everything is always so black and white with him.

I'm surprised when he replies almost instantly. I was sure he wouldn't have bothered at all.

Dan: I take it this is Lily. I'm glad I could help. Good luck with the move. If you need anything, give me a shout. Dan.

Damn it, I probably should have signed off on the text.

There's no reason he would have had my number until now.

Lily: Yeah, it's me. Looks like detective school has finally paid off. 😉

I'm just putting my phone on the bed when it beeps to signal another message. I open it up to see a reply from Dan.

Dan: I've been recapping previous lessons in case you are kidnapped by that Tim or eaten by a cougar.

Lily: You forgot about Mrs Guest's stalker.

Dan: Nah, she'll shoot him and bury the body in her backyard.

I laugh out loud and quickly cover my mouth, hoping not to wake Pops.

Lying on my bed, I text Dan for the next half-hour before falling asleep. I'm excited to wake up and start my new independent life away from the ranch.

Chapter Eight

LILY

It's been a week since I moved off the ranch and into the cabin. I don't think I've had a break since.

Billy, Pops and Luke stuck to their word, and they've been around to help decorate and fix a few bits. Mitch and Dan also came around one day to help with the shed at the back. The whole garden had become overgrown, and it took all of us to work out where my boundary ended. I did call Tim one day to ask him, but he was pretty short with me. It had been a brief conversation, but it was obvious that he was upset with me after believing I was leading him on. I had naively seen him as a friend when I needed one. I never intended to hurt his feelings.

On the other hand, a friend I never thought would support me as much as they have is Dan. Since the first night I started texting him, we have spoken daily, and he's been there on hand whenever Luke or Billy asks him to be. There have been times I wondered if he's doing it for them or me. Silly, I know, as if someone like Dan would be interested in his friend's little sister. That doesn't mean I can't pretend and imagine what it would be like if he was interested. Let's face it: he is a good-looking man, and I have more of a laugh with him than I do with any other guys around here.

I look in the mirror hanging over my sink in my bathroom. I'm exhausted, aching, and longing to climb into bed. But first, I need a long soak in the running bath to ease my tight muscles.

I gather my long black hair into a messy bun before pulling off the clothes I've been wearing when painting and cleaning. My once black leggings and t-shirt are now covered in bleach marks, white paint, and stains from the gloss, wood varnish, and gardening. Who knew renovating an old cabin could be so messy?

I glance at the bathroom window and consider pulling the curtains. No one can see in unless they are good at climbing trees, but since that man has been seen in the woods on more than one occasion, I can't help feeling unsettled. Not that I've admitted that to anyone else.

I look at the window for a moment longer and decide against closing the curtains. Even on a clear night like tonight, the chances of anyone being able to look in through the window are minimal. Plus, if I lie back in the bath and look out the window, I get a lovely clear view of the stars on a clear night. Nothing is more relaxing after a busy day than soaking in the bath and watching the night sky.

I walk over to the large tub and test the temperature of the water before climbing in and slowly sinking into the bubble-filled, lavender-smelling water. Lying back, I close my eyes as the bubbles surround me and help me to relax for the first time all day.

Today, I started turning the basement into my picture-developing room. It is the perfect room for it as there is no natural light, and Pop was able to add a divider wall so I could have a dark room and a studio to paint in. I love taking pictures and printing them to add some paint and make them truly unique.

I've spent nearly the whole day down there putting the finishing touches to everything and finding a home for all my paints, brushes and all the other bits and pieces I will need down there. I also set up a coffee corner, so I don't have to leave the room for a drink. I can't decide if that's a good idea because if I don't have to leave to get coffee, then I will probably forget to eat, which won't go down well with Ma. She's already made me promise to go home at least twice a week for dinner so she can ensure I at least have some decent food in me. I would have considered it an insult, but she makes the others eat dinner at home as much as possible. I think she and Pops will struggle now that we have all moved out of our childhood home.

I take a deep breath as the homesickness starts to kick in. I don't let myself fret about it. I'm sure everyone gets homesick now and again when they first move out. The ranch is the only home I've ever known. I was even born in the house, as were my brothers. Of course, part of me is going to miss it.

I am just sinking a little lower into the water when I hear what sounds like a branch breaking and someone curse. I sit up as my heart races. I shouldn't be hearing anyone out here; there is no one apart from Mrs Guest, and I certainly wouldn't hear anything from her place. I haven't before, anyway.

I listen, paying attention to every sound, but I hear nothing until an owl calls out into the night. I sink back into the water, letting out the breath I was holding. It must have been an owl I heard. Of course, I didn't hear a person. Even Mrs Guest's stalker couldn't see anything out here at night.

The bathroom window lights up as the sensor light is activated, and I jump up again. Oh, come on, Lily. This is getting ridiculous now. I know there are plenty of animals in these woods, I've encountered most of them whilst out taking pictures. Anything could have set off the sensor, something as small as a mouse or as big as a cougar or bear. I need to get a grip on myself.

I climb out of the bath and quickly wrap a towel around me before heading for the bedroom. As I enter, I notice the curtains are open and rush to close them. I know I'm being silly, but I can't shake the unease that started when I was in the bath.

I quickly moisturize and get into my warm pajamas before climbing into bed and unlocking my phone.

The first thing I do is look to see if Dan has messaged, but he hasn't. He has been on call all evening and has probably been called out. I consider messaging or calling him for a moment to see if there have been any more sightings in the woods of the guy Mrs. Guest keeps seeing. But I decide against it last minute. I don't want him to prove that I am being paranoid, and I certainly don't want him to think I'm scared here on my own.

I curl up under the thick blankets and close my eyes, telling myself I have nothing to worry about and that I should get some rest. But sleep doesn't come easy, as the security light keeps coming on, and the animals are very active throughout the night. By the time sunrise comes, I have only dozed on and off and know it's going to be a long day.

Chapter Nine

DAN

What a freaking night!

I was called out just after nine by Mrs Guest, who was convinced she had seen someone sneaking around in the woods again. At this point, we think somebody must be living rough out there, which isn't great as they're a bit close to Lily's cabin for my liking.

I've promised her I won't say anything to her brothers about it, but if I think she's in danger, I will break that promise; I owe her brothers that much. They have done a lot for me over the years, and looking out for their baby sister is the least I can do for them, which is why I was wandering around in those woods over half the night, which wasn't my smartest move. As I know, there are all kinds of animals out there at night, just looking for their next meal. But I had to be sure she was safe.

I'm an idiot, I know. But since I walked in on that sleazeball making her uncomfortable in her own home, I've wanted to protect her and make sure no one made her feel that way again.

I take a sip of my coffee and lean on the table in front of me. I came into the café in town for a big breakfast before heading home to crash out for an hour or two. I'd planned on heading back out to the woods after to see if I could find anything I missed last night. But I'm far too tired. I think I need to pass the baton to someone else on this one. I don't have the expertise like some of my fellow officers. I've never been great at tracking, stupid I know, but it's true.

"Morning Lily, how's the new place?"

I turn my head toward the counter so fast I'm surprised I don't pull something.

"It's great, thanks, Gill. I finally have everything the way I want it," Lily says with her back to me.

"I knew it wouldn't take you long. What can I get you, dear?"

While Lily places her order, I turn back to the table in front of me and try not to let her see I have been eaveswigging her conversation. It doesn't work, though, because as soon as I hear her picking a table number, I look around to see where it is. When I notice it is right next to mine, I get an excited feeling in my gut.

"Morning, Daniel."

I roll my eyes as I turn to see her sitting on the opposite side of the table next to mine, so she's facing me.

"Morning, Lily bear," I reply, grinning. She turns her nose up, as she always does when I call her that. I can't even remember what started it off; it was just a stupid name I called her one day when she was little, and she hated it, so it stuck.

As she picks up her drink to take a sip, I realise she isn't wearing her usual makeup and appears tired. Has she not been sleeping since moving into her place? Is she scared out there alone? Or is there something else keeping her awake, like that guy Tim?

"Can I ask you something?"

I turn to look at Lily and see her chewing on her lip.

"Of course you can," I reply, worried that something is seriously wrong.

"Have there been any more reports of that guy Mrs. Guest has seen a few times?"

I move over to her table and sit down with my mug of coffee before letting out a sigh.

"Yes, she saw him last night. I spent part of the night in the woods looking for him." There's no point lying to her; she obviously knows something about it. "Why do you ask?"

"Because I think he was outside of my place last night."

"What?" I demand, sitting upright in my chair. "Did you see him? Did he approach you?" I demand, but Lily shakes her head.

"No, nothing like that. It was just a feeling I had. Like someone was watching the place, plus the security light kept coming on." She lets out a sigh and rubs her face. "I know I'm probably being silly. It was probably animals setting off the light; I was just on edge, that's all."

I reach across the table and take her hand, needing to offer some comfort.

"Why didn't you call me? I told you, Lil, to call me if you feel scared or need anything. Why didn't you?"

"Because I was sure you would think I was being silly," she says quietly. I shake my head at her in disbelief. I couldn't have been clearer; she was to call me over anything.

"Well, from now on, if you feel unsettled at all, you can call me, okay? I don't care if I'm working; you can call me, and I will check everything out."

Lily nods and looks down at the table, where I realise I'm still holding her hand. I quickly let go, not wanting to make her feel uncomfortable.

My phone beeps in my pocket, and pull it out to see a message from the sheriff.

"I'm sorry, Lils. I have to go." I stand from the chair while finishing my coffee. "Remember, no matter what you are to call me, okay?"

"Okay. Thank you."

I don't know why I do it, but before I can even think, I walk to her side of the table and kiss her cheek.

"Take care of yourself, Lils, and call me if you need me for anything."

She nods as I turn my back to her and start walking out of the café and into the cold winter air.

What the fuck is coming over me? Why did I kiss her like that? Why am I so determined to look after her and keep her safe? There is more to it being because of her brothers. There is a deep need in me to protect her and keep her safe. But what does it mean? Surely it doesn't mean I'm falling for my best friend's sister? Even I'm not that stupid, am I?

Chapter Ten

DAN

I fall onto my sofa and close my eyes. I know I should move to my room, but the thought of getting up feels like too much effort. I have slept very little today, if at all.

While sitting in the café with Lily, I received a message from one of the guys saying Mrs Guest had found something in her garden that shouldn't be there. Of course, I headed straight over and found a black leather glove on the path through the woods leading to Lily's place. There never seems to be a sign of anything when we search. It always seems to be Mrs Guest's word, and that's it.

Our sheriff seems to think it is just someone who walks through the woods at night looking for an escape or to clear their mind. As he said, if they get eaten by anything, then it's their own fault. Everyone knows there are plenty of predators in those woods. There are signs dotted around, just in case people happen to wander in by mistake. But I can't leave this until I know who it is and that Lily is no longer in any form of danger.

I rub my very tired eyes and let out a deep yawn. I can't

even open my eyes, and I'm so tired. Maybe I should sleep here, just for now.

The sound of my mobile ringing makes me jump as I'm dozing off. I groan out loud as I reach for the coffee table, forcing my eyes to open as I fight desperately against sleep.

"Hey?" I sigh without even glancing at the screen to see who's calling.

"Sorry, did I wake you?"

I sit up, suddenly feeling wide awake.

"Lily? No, I was just relaxing. What's the matter? Are you okay?" I ask, already on my feet, gathering my stuff together and getting ready to head to her place.

"I don't know. I think I heard someone trying to get through the front door." I can hear the fear in her voice as I grab my gun and car keys, having already pulled on my boots and coat.

"Where are you?" I ask, walking out of the apartment and heading for my truck.

"In my room. I," she stops mid-sentence, and for a split second, I freeze.

"Lils? What's the matter? What's happened?" I demand, slamming the door shut and starting the engine.

"I thought I heard something," she whispers. Shit, I need to get there.

"Lily, listen to me. I want you to close and lock the bedroom door quietly and stay beside it. If anyone tries to get in, you do what you must to stop them. But stay on the phone with me, okay? I'm on my way."

I hear her creeping through her room, whispering occasionally to let me know she's okay while I drive like a lunatic to get to her.

The usual fifteen-minute journey takes less than ten.

Lily stays on the line the whole time, letting me know she hears very little now.

As I pull up at hers, I see a bear run away from the cabin and wonder if it has been trying to get inside, and that's what she heard.

"I'm outside, Lily. Go to your window and throw the spare key out." I get out of the truck as quietly as possible and rush to the front of the cabin with my gun out. As soon as I'm underneath her window, I see her opening it as quietly as possible and dropping the keys, which I catch. I'm so glad I told her to always keep a set in her room in case of this kind of situation.

I sneak to the front door as quietly as possible and slide the key slowly into the lock. I take one last deep breath to calm my racing heart and focus before throwing open the door with my gun drawn.

As I search the lounge, I see no sign of anyone having been there. I'm starting to think it was the bear trying to get inside as I can smell brisket and know it's a strong enough scent to draw all kinds of wildlife out. That doesn't stop me from thoroughly searching the premises to ensure there isn't anyone hiding. I need to be sure before letting Lily out of the room. But with each room coming up empty, it just confirms that it probably was the bear. By the time I get to Lily's room, I know she'll be in a panic.

"It's me, Lil. Open up," I call through the door and hear the key turn in the lock before it opens. She stands before me, crying. I put the safety on my weapon and place it on the chest of drawers by the door before pulling her into my arms. She shakes as she cries quietly in my arms.

"You're okay, sweetheart. No one's here," I whisper into her hair as I hold her head against my chest, needing to reassure myself that she's safe and in no danger.

"I can't believe I called you because of my own stupid imagination," she sniffs into my shirt. I take hold of her head and hold it in place as I lean back to look at her.

"I'm glad that you called me. I was able to check everything out and ensure you weren't in any danger. I don't care if you call me every night, as long as you are safe." I look deep into her brown, tear-filled eyes as she nods and pull her back against me so I can hold her until she starts feeling safe again.

After a short time, Lily pulls away from me and we head downstairs. I can see her looking around, reassuring herself that no one's here. She's still on edge. I know there's no way I can leave yet as she won't relax.

"Come on, let's get you a hot drink to see if it helps you to settle."

Lily nods and follows me into the kitchen, where I tell her to sit at the breakfast bar while I make us both a drink. She feels much more awake than before she called me. I know I will have trouble sleeping tonight as I want to know she's safe.

"So, there was nothing there? I imagined everything?" she asks as I put the kettle on to boil.

"When I arrived, a bear ran past the building and into the woods. I think it was drawn to the place from the smell coming from inside," I smile as I nod towards the slow cooker on the side. "To be fair, that smells amazing! Brisket?" I watch Lily nod before turning my back to her to get two mugs out of the cupboard. Thankfully, I watched her make us all drinks the other day when I was here and remembered where everything is. "I love brisket; it's one of my favourites."

"I'll make it for you one day to say thank you."

I turn to look at her and smile.

"I would like that."

We remain silent for the next few minutes as I finish making the drinks before passing one to her. I watch as she pours honey into her black tea as she always does and decide to copy her, to give it a try. I'm surprised how much better it tastes than sugar.

"I'm sorry for calling you out. This whole thing with Mrs Guest has gotten to me more than I was willing to admit," she sighs, looking into her mug. I reach over and place a hand on hers, which is resting on the top.

"I'm glad you are paying attention and keeping yourself safe. It's important to be aware of your surroundings out here."

She looks up at me and nods.

"Thank you, Dan, for being so understanding. I didn't want to call my family, as they would say they told me so and force me to return to the ranch."

I give her hand one last squeeze before forcing myself to let go.

"That's why I gave you my number and told you to message or ring anytime. That still stands."

We sit in silence for a bit as we both drink our drinks. The closer I get to emptying my mug, the more I realise I don't want to leave. I can see she's tired, but she's also so on edge that she isn't going to sleep. I make an instant decision and don't let myself look too into it.

"Would you feel better if I slept on the sofa tonight?" I offer. When Lily looks up, I smile. "I know you will try to argue, but you're exhausted and need a decent nights sleep. Me being downstairs will help you relax enough to sleep properly." I watch as she thinks about it for a moment before giving me a slight nod.

"Are you sure you don't mind? My couch isn't exactly comfortable," she starts, but I cut her off with a smile.

"Of course, I don't mind. Now let's get everything locked up, and then you can go off to bed, and we can both get some shut-eye."

We spent the next five minutes ensuring everything was secure to put Lily's mind at ease. She also made sure to get me everything I may need and more. There is no way I will need this many blankets and pillows, but if it makes her feel better to make a fuss, I'll let her. In the end, though, I put my foot down and told her to go to bed so I could lie on the couch and close my eyes.

Sleep doesn't find me easily. As I lay with one arm behind my head, I can't stop analysing everything that happened tonight. Not the actual incident, but how I felt from the moment I realised it was Lily on the phone and she might be in danger.

As much as I try to ignore it, there's no mistaking that Lily has stopped being just my best friend's little sister in the last couple of weeks. She's become more, and I don't know how to feel about it. I know Luke and Billy would literally kill me if they found out I had romantic feelings for her, but I can't help it. She's intelligent, funny, and beautiful. She's no longer the stick of a girl who made it her sole purpose to annoy the hell out of us. Somehow, she has become someone I want to spend time with, and I enjoy those moments far more than I should.

I close my eyes, thinking of the woman upstairs and try to push back all the confusing thoughts racing through my mind as I try to get some much-needed sleep. Maybe, just maybe, these feelings will disappear soon, as they usually do when I start to like a woman. Lily may be different from all the other women I have met, but she isn't that different, is she?

Chapter Eleven

LILY

I wake up to the sun shining through the open curtains. I stretch before climbing out of the bed and stretch again. I can't remember the last time I slept that well. I walk to the window and see Dan's truck still parked where he left it last night. Shit, I forgot all about him for a second.

I still can't believe he came running like he did. I called, and he was here within ten minutes, searching my home, armed and ready to protect me. I have to keep reminding myself he was doing his job and that he didn't treat me any differently than he would have any other woman alone in the woods if they called him. But then he slept over, and I'm pretty sure he wouldn't do that for just anyone, would he?

I grab my robe and wrap it around myself before slowly sneaking out of the room and towards the stairs, hoping not to wake him if he's still asleep. The couch comes into view halfway down the stairs, and I see him still fast asleep on the sofa. He looks so peaceful and relaxed that I consider going back up the stairs to my room and leaving him in peace for a while longer. Unfortunately, I have a client to meet today about some of my prints being sold at their auction. I can't afford not to make that meeting.

I slowly make my way down the rest of the stairs and past the sofa before heading into the kitchen. I need a mug of coffee before I start to get ready. I make it past the couch without waking him and close the kitchen door behind me. I sneak a peek at him while closing it. He looks so comfortable with the blankets up to his neck as he sleeps soundly. His brown hair is messier than I've seen it before, and strangely, it suits him that way.

I go about making us both a coffee, knowing that I will need to wake him, as I'm sure he'll have to be at work at some point today. I make a point of getting the best coffee, as he deserves it after coming to my rescue last night.

I walk over to the door with both mugs in one hand as I open it, expecting Dan to still be asleep on the sofa. Instead, I find him on his feet, stretching, in nothing but a tight pair of boxers. His back is to me, giving me the chance to admire the way his muscles flex and ripple. Shit, when did he get so fit?

Dan turns around suddenly, catching me staring at him like a crazed stalker.

"Uh, morning. I made coffee," I stammer, holding up the mugs. A smirk spreads across his face, and I know he saw me checking him out.

"Thanks, Lily bear," he chuckles, stepping forward and taking the mug from me. I roll my eyes but don't bother arguing over the nickname. Do I like it now? It makes me feel special that he has a name for me, but I'm sure he has a name for all the women he has slept with over the years because I know there have been a lot of them.

That thought quickly snaps me from the tiny fantasy I've lived in since he came to my rescue last night. He doesn't see me as anything more than his best friend's sister. He could have any woman he wanted; why would he want someone six years younger than him?

"What do you have planned for today?" he asks as he takes a sip of his drink before placing it on the coffee table and retrieving his shirt from the back of the chair where he put his clothes last night. I try not to watch as he pulls it over his head, but it's like fighting a losing battle with my own eyes. I can't tear them away from the view in front of me. This time, he doesn't catch me looking as I turn my attention to the window before he looks over his shoulder.

"I've gotta go over to the next town. I have a meeting with the art gallery there," I reply as I look back at the now fully-dressed Dan. "What about you? Are you working?"

Dan nods as he downs his coffee.

"Yeah, I better get going; otherwise, I'll be late." He looks at me and smiles. "Thanks for the coffee, Lils."

"It's the least I can do after all you did for me last night," I reply, placing my mug on the coffee table and heading to the door with him. As he opens the front door, I tighten the robe around me, and the cold morning air flows in.

"I told you, it was no problem. Never worry about calling me. If you feel unsafe, you do exactly what you did last night."

I nod, not looking at him, as I know he wouldn't want me to call him whenever I get scared. He will eventually get sick of it. Dan reaches out, hooks a finger under my chin, and applies pressure, forcing me to lift my head so I'm looking into his blue eyes.

"I'm serious, Lily. I don't care if I sleep on your couch every night for as long as it takes you to feel safe. You can call me whenever you need me, okay?"

I'm taken aback by the intensity in his eyes.

"Okay," I reply quietly as my throat tightens. Dan lets go of my chin and looks like he still doesn't believe me, but he's accepting my word for now.

"Good. Now I need to go. Have a good day." He surprises me by pulling me into his arms, holding me tight as I feel myself relaxing into him. His scent overpowers me and causes me to shiver with need. He smells so damn good. Dan kisses my head before letting me go and stepping out of the door.

"I will call you tonight to see how you're feeling. But if you need me before then, message or call me." He jogs down the front steps and turns with a smile, which falters as he stares at me. For a moment, our eyes met, and I'm frozen to the spot. Dan seems to come to his senses and shakes his head before heading to his truck.

"See you later, Lily bear!" he calls, laughing as he jumps into his car and backs down the dirt drive. I wave as he disappears and close the door before locking it.

What the hell is going on with us? Why has he suddenly changed from my brother's annoying friend to someone I want around? Shit, this isn't good. I'm going to fall for the guy, and he isn't even interested in me back. Or is he? I get so many mixed signals from him that I don't know what's real and what is all in my head.

I pull my phone out of my robe pocket and go to message Elli to see if she is free for a chat, but I stop myself. I can't go to her. What if she tells Luke? He would go mad if he knew I had not only called Dan instead of him last night but that I'd started developing feelings for the guy.

I take a deep breath as I collect my mug on the way to my room and try to work out why life has to be so goddamn complicated.

Chapter Twelve

DAN

Fuck, I can't concentrate on anything today, my head is all over the place. After this morning, there's no mistaking my feelings for Lily. For a moment, when I was walking away from her place, I turned around and saw her standing in the doorway. I wondered what it would be like if that were an everyday occurrence. If she waved me off to work each morning and was there waiting for me to finish?

I shake my head as the image of her standing there in her robe invades my thoughts for the umpteenth time today. I know I need to distance myself from her, but I have to make sure she is safe first. I can't do that until I find out why someone keeps being seen in an area of the woods so close to hers. Where are they coming from, and are they even going anywhere near her place?

"Hey, you got a second, Dan?"

I turn to see the sheriff walking towards my desk.

"Sure, what's up?" I ask, glad to have something to distract me from a certain little lady.

"I've just had the insurance company on the phone—

the ones that deal with Gerald's robbery," he explains as he leans back against the edge of my desk and crosses his arms and legs in front of him. They think it was an inside job and want to know my opinions on it."

"Do *you* think it was an inside job?" I ask, frowning.

"Do I think Gerald robbed his own place of petty cash? Hell no! I've known that guy as long as I've been alive. He is as straight as an arrow. There's no way he would try something like this."

I frown at the Sheriff as I lean back in my seat and cross my arms over my chest.

"Then what do you need me for if you are so sure he's innocent?" I ask. The sheriff scratches at his thick beard, a nervous tick he has, which tells me he thinks there's more to this and doesn't like it.

"What do you know of his son?"

"Tim?" I ask, and an instant distaste fills my mouth. "I don't really know him personally, just because of who his old man is." The fact that he obviously has a thing for Lily makes her uncomfortable. I don't know if he has been in touch with her since that day I turned up at her place. I need to ask her.

"Do you think he could have tried to rob the place?" Sheriff Hobbs asks. I rub the back of my neck.

"From what I know of the guy, he isn't the smartest, and he did seem a little off when asked if he knew the safe had been emptied the night before." Especially when I mentioned it at Lily's; maybe the sheriff is onto something with this. "Did Gerald ever say why he emptied the safe that night? Apparently, it was something he didn't usually do," I point out. The sheriff shakes his head.

"No, that's what the insurance company mentioned as well. When they asked Gerald, he just said he wasn't sure;

he just did it without thinking. He claims it was a sixth sense, hocus pocus bullshit."

"But you're not convinced?" I ask. The sheriff shakes his head again before letting out a deep breath. "Do you want me to dig around and see what I can come up with regarding the son?" I offer.

"If you could, see what your friends know about him. He's only a couple of years younger than you; surely someone you know must know him."

I take a deep breath and sit up straight, moving my chair closer to my desk.

"Leave it with me. I'll see what I can dig up."

The Sheriff claps me on the shoulder before standing up from the desk.

"I knew I could count on you. Thanks, Deputy." He walks away as I pick up my phone and check for the umpteenth time if Lily has messaged. When I see the blank screen, I decide to investigate Tim Gerald and see what I can come up with.

"And you don't know where your son is?" I ask Mr Gerald, who shakes his head.

"Why do you need to speak to Timothy? What's he been accused of now?" he asks, causing me to frown.

"Is it normal for Tim to get accused of things?" I ask. Mr Gerald seems to realise himself and quickly shakes his head.

"Of course not. He's a good boy and a big help to me." I can tell instantly he has gone on the defensive, and I won't get anything meaningful from him now. It's late in the day anyway, and I should be clocking off soon. I plan on checking in on Lily before settling down for the night.

The bell above the front door rings, and I see Tim strolling into the office.

"Hey, Deputy Thomas. What are you doing here?" he asks, trying to appear calm and collected, but I don't miss how his step falters when he spots me.

"I was looking for you, actually. I was wondering if you wouldn't mind answering a few questions about the break-in. The insurance company wants us to confirm a few things, and I don't want to do anything until I'm completely sure my notes are correct," I lie. Tim instantly starts rubbing his neck and looking around as if for an excuse to be anywhere but here.

"Uh, yeah, sure. I have a few spare minutes," he says, walking around one of the desks and sitting in the chair. He waves his hand to the seat opposite. He's trying to push his dominance by sitting in the 'powerful' seat behind the desk, not in front of it. I don't fall for this playground bullshit. I've been an officer too long to miss a power play like this. Instead, I walk to the same side of the desk as him and lean back against it, ensuring I'm taller than him, showing him who is really in charge here.

"You said you were in bed around the time of the break-in. I take it there are no witnesses," I say, reading through my notes in my notepad, even though I know the details off the top of my head.

"No, I was alone. But Pa had seen me going to bed. Isn't that right, Pa?" Tim calls across the office. I look over my shoulder and see Mr Gerald nodding, but he's frowning slightly. He never saw his son going to bed that night. But I can't call him out on it just yet, not without proof. The fucker Tim is guilty as sin, and I need to prove it.

"And you were still in bed when your father told you about the break-in?" I ask, once again pretending to read the information from the notebook.

"That's right."

I smile at him and stand from the desk.

"Then that's all I need to tell the insurance company. Hopefully, they will get off all our backs, and you will get your payout," I say, looking between them. "I'm sorry to have bothered you both."

"That's fine; you are only doing your job," Tim says, smiling as he holds out his hand. I reluctantly shake it before going over to his father and shaking his.

"That I am. Hopefully, it will all be over and in the past for you soon," I say, turning to the door. I purposely open the door to make them think I am leaving before turning back around to face them.

"One thing," I start, which causes both to stare at me. There is no mistaking the panicked look Mr Gerald throws in his son's direction for a moment before remembering himself. "Why did you get the insurance company involved? I thought it was only loose change that was taken?" I ask, looking between the two of them. Tim quickly looks at his father, who looks at me and shrugs.

"The accountant insisted on it; he's trying to get me compensated for the damage to the fire exit door from where they broke in as well as the two days' earnings." I can tell instantly that the story has been practised. Mr Gerald isn't as good at acting when under inspection. His son was involved, and he knows or at least suspects it.

"That makes sense. Thanks for clearing that up," I say, forcing a big smile. Tim smirks back at me, obviously thinking he has gotten away with it.

"If you need to know anything else, please feel free to

come back." The smug bastard thinks he's gotten off scot-free, and I can't wait to arrest the fucker. I continue to smile as I go to walk out of the door. "Oh, and say hi to Lily for me. I love what she's done with the cabin."

This time, I spin around and look at him. When I do, I notice mud around the bottom of his boots. It's not rained in days; the only wet ground is areas under trees where the sun can't reach to speed up the drying process, like in the woods around Lily's.

"I promised to call her later, so I can pass on the message," I reply, not missing the way his smile falls from his face. I grin as I walk away and head for my police cruiser. I need to get to my truck and to Lily's as quickly as possible to check that all is okay, as something tells me it's not.

Chapter Thirteen

LILY

I pull onto the dirt road leading to the cabin and sigh, glad to get home. The meeting did not go as planned, and they only wanted two of the five pieces I hoped they would sell for me. I will still make a fair bit from their chosen pieces, but I could have done with them taking all five.

I stop outside my place and look at the outside of my home. Even with everything that happened last night, I'm still so glad I found this place when I did.

My phone starts to ring as I shut off the engine, and I find myself smiling when I see Dan's name flash on the screen. I've been trying not to think about him all day and failed miserably.

"Haven't you seen enough of me recently? I would have thought you'd be avoiding me at all costs," I tease as I climb out of the car. I hear his rich laugh down the line, which fills me with warmth.

"I thought maybe it was the other way around," he chuckles. "How did it go today? Are you a millionaire yet?"

I can hear that he's driving, and for a moment, I hope he's heading here.

"No, such luck. They didn't want it all, only two pieces," I sigh.

"I'm sorry, Lily bear. If it's any consolation, it's their loss."

I find myself smiling as it's what I need to hear. I walk up the porch steps whilst finding the right key. I unlock the door and walk in, expecting it to be warmer than outside, but it's not. If anything, it's colder.

"What the hell?" I mutter as I feel a draft coming from the kitchen.

"Everything okay? Where are you?" I hear Dan ask.

"I just got home," I answer, walking into the kitchen, where I find the source of the draft. "The back door's open," I tell Dan as I start to panic. I know I didn't unlock that door this morning. Dan and I checked it together last night before we went to sleep.

"What do you mean? Lily? What's going on?" I hear Dan demanding as I spin around and expect to see someone standing behind me, but there's no one.

"Someone's been in here," I say as I slowly make my way to the front door, scared to turn my back on any open space in case someone jumps out and grabs me from behind.

"Shit. Get out now! I'm nearly there." I can hear the worry in his voice, which doesn't help my anxiety. I turn around and run out of the door, looking around, expecting someone to be there.

I hear a car approaching at speed and turn just in time to see Dan race into view in his truck. He screeches to a stop beside my car and jumps out, his gun already in his hand.

"Get over here!" he snaps, waving me over to him. As soon as I'm beside him, he points for me to get behind the wheel. Once I'm sat inside, he leans in.

"Lock the doors and stay in here, no matter what you see or hear. Do not get out of this vehicle unless I tell you to."

"Be careful," I whisper as he goes to close the door. I can feel my whole body shaking, not only from the cold. Dan looks at me for a moment before leaning in and pressing a kiss to my forehead.

"Don't worry about me."

"But I do," I reply. He looks at me for a moment, as if shocked, before giving me a small smile as he stands and closes the door. He locks the truck with the fob before heading to my place, gun in hand. I watch as he listens with caution by the front door before entering.

The chances of anyone still being in there are minimal, especially as they would have heard me enter and Dan arrive. But that doesn't stop me from holding my breath, as I know Dan is inside and may not be alone.

Seconds feel like hours as I watch the cabin for any sign of what's happening inside. I can't stop the deep shaking that's taking over my body. I feel useless sitting here whilst Dan puts his life on the line for me. I know it's his job, but it still feels wrong.

I don't know how long I sit, watching, waiting, but eventually, Dan walks out of the cabin, tucking his gun into its holster. He still seems alert as he walks towards the truck, looking towards the trees on either side of us. As he reaches me, he opens the door and holds out a hand to help me out. He pulls me straight into his arms and holds me tight as I rest my head on his broad chest.

"The place is empty. It doesn't look like anything is missing, but you will need to double-check. I noticed muddy footprints in the kitchen," he says into my hair as I feel myself relax.

"I didn't unlock that door after we locked up last night," I reply into his chest. I hear Dan sigh as his arms tighten around me.

"Come on, let's check that everything is still there, and then we can decide what to do next." Dan puts an arm around my shoulders and leads me towards the cabin.

I look up at the building as we approach and feel myself shudder. Dan's arm tightens around me as we enter, and I start looking around the lounge in front of me.

Everything looks exactly as I left it. Nothing seems to be missing or out of place. The TV and laptop I used before leaving are still there. As we go from room to room, I confirm that nothing is missing. Footprints lead from the kitchen into the lounge. We aren't sure if they stopped there or if the mud just rubbed off. I haven't mopped the floors in the last few days, so they could have been left by me and Dan yesterday, and we didn't notice. Do I believe that? I don't know. I want to as the alternative is that someone has been in my home while I was out.

"Maybe they had just gotten in when they heard me coming home?" I suggest, but Dan doesn't seem convinced.

"Whatever happened, I'm just glad you didn't get hurt," he says as he tightens his hold on my hand for a moment before stepping away and running his hand through his hair. "I don't like the idea of you being alone tonight." He turns to look at me for a moment. "I'm going to stay on the couch again." Before I can say anything, he takes my hand and leads me to the kitchen, where he locks the door and leaves the key in the lock instead of hanging it on a hook like I usually do. He retakes my hand and leads me out of the cabin, locking the front door behind us.

"Where are you taking me?" I ask, following him to the truck. He doesn't answer but holds the passenger door open and watches as I climb in. "Dan?" but it falls on deaf ears. He closes the door and walks quickly to his side before climbing behind the wheel.

"Are you going to tell me where we are going?" I demand as he starts the engine and backs down the dirt road away from mine.

"We'll park down the road, then walk back. Whoever it is may try to come back if they think I've left," he explains, turning off the road and pulling into a dark, overgrown lot that doesn't look like it's been used in years.

"Then why am I here? I could have waited for you at my place?" I point out. But as the truck comes to a stop, Dan turns his attention to me, and I freeze from the seriousness in his eyes.

"Do you really think I would risk leaving you alone in that place now? Not happening, Lily bear. You are staying where I can keep an eye on you."

I don't know what to say or how to feel. This isn't the Dan I've grown up with. This is a different side to him that I know I like far more than I should. But it doesn't stop the warm feeling that grows when I realise he's protecting and taking care of me when I need him the most.

Dan doesn't say anything else. Instead, he climbs out of the truck and retrieves a bag from his truck bed while I leave the cab and stand beside him, waiting to head home. The evening air is colder than I realised, and in Dan's haste to leave, I never grabbed my jacket from the car, where I had left it earlier.

Dan closes the back of the truck and holds out his police jacket.

"Put your arms in here; you look freezing," he sighs, placing it around my shoulders when I don't move to comply. "I don't need it right now, you do. Now put your arms in."

I do as he says and instantly feel swamped by the oversized jacket. The smell of him fills my senses and I pretend to huddle inside to keep warm, when in reality, I'm smelling his aftershave from the material as he zips up the jacket for me.

Dan picks up his bag in one hand and takes my hand in the other as soon as I pull it from the sleeve. He leads me away from the truck and through the woods, in the direction of my place. When he doesn't let go, I keep quiet, enjoying the feel of his big hand around my small one.

"What's in the bag? Secret detective stuff?" I ask, flashing Dan a cheeky smile, hoping to lighten the mood.

"Only if secret detective stuff is code for clean clothes and toiletries," he replies, smiling back as I look at the bag and frown.

"Do you always carry an overnight bag?"

Dan doesn't look at me as he shakes his head.

"No, I packed it this morning, just in case. It's a good job I did." There's a seriousness in his voice that makes me wonder if he had been hoping he wouldn't need it. Who could blame him?

"Sorry," I whisper, looking down at the ground. I feel his hand tighten around mine as he forces me to stop. I look up to find him frowning.

"What on earth have you got to be sorry for?"

I look down at my feet as I push some fallen leaves around.

"The last thing you wanted was to babysit your friend's sister," I mumble.

"Look at me," Dan commands, and I find myself doing as asked. "I am not babysitting you; I'm protecting you, there is a big difference."

"Same thing," I sigh quietly, looking away. Dan drops his bag and places a hooked finger under my chin, forcing me to look back at him.

"It's not the same thing, and you know it. I wouldn't be anywhere else right now, Lily. All I can think about is you and keeping you safe." Dan moves his hand and cups my cheek. "Your safety is all that matters to me," he says as he runs a thumb over my cheek. "*You* are all that matters to me."

I close my eyes and enjoy the feeling of him being so close because I have no idea when it will happen again.

"Thank you," I sigh as I open my eyes, and he steps away.

"You don't need to thank me, not for watching over you."

Dan picks up his bag, and we walk back to the house in silence as I try to convince myself I'm not falling for this man.

Chapter Fourteen

DAN

I lie awake, staring at the lounge ceiling. My thoughts too chaotic to let me rest.

What the hell am I doing? It's like I can't stop myself from making this huge mistake. But is it a mistake? Sure, Luke and Billy will think it is, but do their views really matter here? So, what if I've fallen for their baby sister? At least with me, they will know she's protected. Because there sure as hell isn't anything I wouldn't do to keep her safe. I'm sleeping on her sofa, with my gun to hand, for Christ's sake; what more do I need to do?

How about admitting you're falling for Lily and doing something about it?

I sigh, placing my arms over my eyes. Since when have I been this pathetic with women? Maybe it's because Lily isn't an ordinary woman; she's unique in so many ways. Spending time with her as I have the last few days has confirmed that the girl I watched grow up is now an intelligent, vibrant, beautiful young woman, and I've never met anyone like her before.

There is also the reason that I'm lying here in the middle of the night.

Everything tells me that Tim is coming into her house. I have no idea why, other than it was apparent he had developed feelings for her. There is also the comment made by his father that is playing on my mind. What complaints have been made about Tim in the past? Are they related to the break-in? Or are the complaints made by women? Has he broken into someone's house before to scare them, or worse? I need to look into his record and see what comes up. But I haven't had the chance as so much has happened since I paid him and his father a visit.

A coyote calls in the night, but it's not that which catches my attention. I lie perfectly still as I hear something walking across the gravel on the driveway. It's moving too slowly and deliberately for it to be a bear or any other creature that lives in these woods. I continue to listen as the wooden boards of the front porch creak. Laying further down on the couch to ensure I'm not seen I hear the footsteps stop by the window. Thankfully, it's not too hard for me to hide as they will only see the back of the sofa. I listen carefully as they move from the window towards the back of the building. There's no way I'd have heard them if I'd been asleep, but thankfully, I'm awake and ready.

As the footsteps move further around the side of the building, I realise they're going to the back door. They have already gotten in once; it's time to see how they managed it.

I climb off the sofa quietly and slide on my boots before grabbing my gun and moving to a better spot. As I stand by the kitchen, being sure to stay away from any windows, I spot something moving on the stairs. I look up to see Lily standing there in nothing but some pajamas bottoms and a T-shirt. I hold up my hand to stop her before pressing a finger to my lips, signalling her to stay quiet. I quickly point back up the stairs towards her room and signal a locking motion praying she will understand what I want her to do. Thankfully, she turns and rushes silently back up the stairs and towards her room. I try to listen out for the sound of her door locking, but the sound of someone approaching the back door catches my attention instead.

I could open the door, jump out and arrest them, but I'll have no case without them actively entering the property. I need to let them get inside, so there's no doubt they intended to do so.

I hear the key slowly sliding into the lock on the back door, and it just confirms my suspicions on how they are getting in. They have a set of their own keys. I bet Tim had a set cut before handing them over to Lily. It's that, or he kept a set for himself.

The sound of the locking mechanism slowly turning and clicking out of place, fills the silence before the handle turns and the door creaks open so slightly. But before I can approach or jump out at them, the light of a torch shines through the gap and bounces off my gun, alerting them of my presence.

"Fuck!" I curse as the door slams shut before I can get to it. I throw it open, but they've already made it down to the garden path and are a good distance away. That doesn't stop me from racing after them, though. They won't get away from me now; I have them within my grasp.

I'm a fit man; I work out nearly every day and run three or four times a week. I hope that will mean I can catch them before they get too far into the woods. It's a cloudy night, so there is no light out here. I only have a short time to catch the guy and make my girl safe.

I continue to run as fast as I can, but it's not easy when

you can't see the broken twigs and leaves under your feet. From what I can tell, I think it's a male with a similar build to Tim Gerald, but I can't confirm it without seeing his face. They may just be wearing a bulky jacket; it's hard to tell what's clothing and what's their physique.

I'm losing them; I know I am. It's not safe out here to be chasing after someone, and they are using that fact to their advantage.

There is one more thing to try.

"Stop, or I'll shoot!" I call out, lifting my gun and firing one warning shot into the air. But they disappear into the thicker trees, and I lose them. As they do, I glimpse their arm as they pass through an area where the moonlight is penetrating and see what looks like a tattoo. But they are gone before I can see anything else or the details. Running off into the dark woods.

"Fuck!" I curse as I force myself to stop. They've beaten me, and we both know it. "You won't get away next time!" I call out! "Come near her or her place again, and you are a dead man. Mark my words!" I yell as I pocket my gun and listen to see if they are close, but I can't hear anything other than typical nighttime sounds.

"Fuck!" I curse again as I turn around and hope I'm heading in the right direction to Lily's house.

I jog lightly back, hoping she's still locked in her room. The need to see she's okay propels me forward, and even through the dark woods, her place comes into sight. I jog to the back door and open it, listening for any sound coming from the inside. There is no way they could have double-backed and beat me here, but it doesn't stop me from being cautious.

"Lily, it's safe!" I call out as I close the door and lock it.

"Dan?" I hear her call back quickly, followed by a door

opening and her running down the stairs. I walk through the kitchen door into the lounge as she throws herself at me, wrapping her arms around my neck. I hold her tight, breathing in her sweet jasmine shower gel and moisturiser. The scent calms my racing mind as I remind myself she's safe, even if only for now.

Lily steps back and starts looking me over.

"I heard a shot. Are you hurt? Did they shoot at you?" she asks, checking for a gunshot wound. I take her hands and press them between mine before kissing her knuckles.

"I'm fine; it was me who fired the gun," I explain, leaving my lips against her fingers. "It was a warning shot, but I will get them next time." I look into her eyes whilst placing a hand on her cheek. "I won't stop until I know you are safe," I whisper, running my thumb under her eye, wiping away the tears leaking from them.

For a moment, I look deep into her brown eyes, and everything I have been worried about ceases to exist. All that matters now is that she's safe and here with me. I don't stop to think as I lean in and place a soft kiss on her lips. I don't know what I expect to happen, but it isn't for her to wrap her arms around my neck and kiss me back. It takes less than a second for my body to take over, and I wrap my arms around her waist and hold her tight to me.

Lily takes hold of my t-shirt and pulls me with her as she moves us to the sofa. We continue to kiss as she turns us around, forcing me to sit on the sofa. She straddles my lap and continues to kiss me with her fingers threaded into my hair. I'm rock-hard underneath her and know she can feel it as she grinds against my lap.

"Is this what you want?" I ask, lifting my hips. She gasps as her head falls back. I keep one hand on her hips and the other on the top of her back as she rocks against my raised hips again.

"Yes," she sighs, sitting up straight and looking at me with the perfect 'come fuck me' eyes. "Take me to bed, Dan."

I don't need telling twice. I grab her ass and lift her with me as my lips find hers again.

I carry her through the lounge and up the stairs, only briefly allowing our lips to part before kissing her again on the landing until we reach her room. I walk through the door and lay her down on her big bed so I'm in between her legs. I lift away slightly and smile, looking into her eyes.

"Is this what you really want, Lily Bear?" I ask, running my knuckles over her cheek as she nods. "Good," is all I say before my lips crash into hers again.

I continue to kiss her as I pull her into a sitting position and make short work of pulling her top off. I silently thank God that she hasn't worn a bra to bed as her perfect perky breasts come into view. I cup one as I take its nipple between my thumb and forefinger, testing how sensitive they are. When Lily lets out the sweetest moan, I grin to myself before taking one between my teeth.

"Dan."

The sound of my name on her lips as she moans is my new personal aphrodisiac. I moan around her nipple as my cock hardens to the point it's painful. The need to taste more of her overcomes me as I start kissing around her breasts before moving down her stomach and between her legs.

I take hold of the elastic of her pajama bottoms and look up to her beautiful face.

"Lift your hips for me, sweetheart," I whisper, my voice

deep with need. Lily does as I ask, and in seconds, I have her completely naked before me.

I look down at the beautiful angel lying on the bed. Her long dark hair surrounds her head like a halo in the dark. How can one person bring so much light to a dark room? Even in the dark of night, all I can see is her beauty, and it's mesmerising.

I press a kiss to her stomach as my finger slides gently between her perfect folds. She's so wet and smells so sweet.

"Dan, please."

I look up from where I'm still kissing her lower stomach as my finger finds her clit.

"Is this what you need, Lily bear?" I ask whilst circling her clit gently.

"More," she gasps as I rub it a little harder.

"More?" I repeat as I rub a little harder again and faster.

"Yes! More!" she moans as she lifts her hips to meet me and tell me exactly what she needs.

"How about this?" I bury my face between her legs as I push a finger into her, testing what she can take.

"Yes," Lily cries out as I flick my tongue over her clit and add a second finger. I smile to myself as her flavour explodes on my tongue. She tastes better than anyone I've ever tasted before.

I continue to tease and lick her, edging her three or four times until she is crying out for me to let her come. I love the sound of her begging and how well she can take it. I'm not being gentle now; the need to hear her cry out has taken over, and I fucking love the way my name sounds as she cries out.

"Come for me, baby girl," I growl in a voice I don't even recognise as I push her over the edge.

She screams my name as she climaxes and shudders around my fingers. I can't wait to feel that around my cock as I make her come whilst buried deep inside her.

I slowly remove my fingers from her and suck them clean as I kiss up her stomach, giving her time to recover slightly before I take her completely.

By the time my lips finally reach hers, Lily is nearly feral with need again. She threads her fingers into my hair and kisses me with a passion I haven't felt before. Her tongue invades my mouth, and I accept it willingly. I position myself at her entrance. I'm so hard I don't need any assistance finding where I want to be.

"Lily?" I beg against her lips.

"Fuck me, Dan. Please."

I thrust into her, and we both cry out. I force myself to stay still for a moment, knowing I will blow my load in seconds if I move too much. She is so perfect, too perfect for me, but now I have her, and I know I'll never let her go.

Slowly, I gain control of my body as I move within her. Lily wraps her legs around my waist, pulling me deeper within her as she cries out with pleasure.

"Oh shit, don't stop," she begs as I grind into her, feeling her from the inside out. I couldn't stop if I wanted to. A primal need within makes me lean my head down to her shoulder and bite down, sucking her flesh into my mouth, needing to leave my mark on her, so everyone will know she is mine.

"Fuck," she cries out into the silent night as she clamps my cock so hard I swear I will lose it. That's fine. I want it buried deep inside her for the rest of her life so no one can take her again. I will ruin her for all other men. Because now I've had her, there will be no other for her, whether she likes it or not.

I'm wild now with the primal need to fill her with my release. I'm usually more careful than this, I don't fuck women bareback, but I don't want anything coming between me and this amazing woman underneath me. I need to feel all of her, inside and out.

The only sounds in the night now are the sounds of the bed, the slapping sound of wet flesh as I pound into her, and our deep breathing as we moan together in pure pleasure. I hope whoever tried to get in here can hear the way I'm making her moan. She is mine, and he will never get near her.

"Fuck!" I cry out as I thrust into her hard and explode as she climaxes again.

As I fall beside her and pull her into my arms, I know I'm well and truly in the shit. Feeling her naked and gasping for breath against my chest as we both recover from what may have been the best sex I have ever had, I know that there is no way I can let her go again. Tomorrow, when we are both thinking a little more clearly, I'm going to tell her that this isn't a one-night thing for me. Lily Johnson is mine, and I have no plans of ever letting her go.

Chapter Fifteen

LILY

I wake up to birds singing outside the window and a hard chest under my head. I'm lying with my head on Dan's chest as he runs his fingers up and down my bare arm, leaving a tingling sensation in its wake.

"You okay, Lily bear?" he asks quietly. I nod into his chest and look up at him, smiling.

"I never thought I would like you calling me that."

Dan smiles as he leans in and kisses the end of my nose.

"I like that you finally approve because it seems weird calling you anything else these days," he replies, smiling as he leans back with one arm behind his head. Before letting out a deep sigh. "Your brothers are going to kill me."

I laugh as I lean back a little, lying on the pillow beside him.

"Do they have to know?" I have no idea what this is between us and don't want to be overbearing and ask him. When Dan turns his head, I can't miss the huge smile on his face.

"I think they're going to notice when I keep coming

around and can't keep my hands to myself." He leans in and kisses my lips. "I don't want this to be a one-time thing, do you?" he asks, his lips brushing against mine every so lightly.

"No," I whisper back truthfully.

"Good." Dan's lips find mine as his fingers thread into the hair at the back of my head. I kiss him for a few minutes, loving how his lips feel against mine when he reluctantly pulls away from me and looks at the window.

"I have to get ready for work. I also want to look through the woods and see if your little visitor left any clues behind," he climbs out of bed as I sit up and wrap my arms around my legs, bringing them up to my chest. I watch as Dan walks across the bedroom completely naked. His well-trained body has dips and curves in all the right places. When the morning light shines off his toned back, I almost forget the fear that sits in my gut.

"Do you think he will come back?"

When Dan turns to look at me, I can see I won't like the answer.

"Something keeps drawing him back." He picks up his boxers from the floor at the bottom of the bed and pulls them on before turning his attention back to me. "I'm pretty sure that something is you."

I let out a sigh and hug my legs closer to my chest.

"I need to go back to the ranch, don't I." It's not a question; I know I do. "I wanted this place so much, and I never thought I would be in any danger here other than the cougar." I close my eyes and lean my forehead on my knees. The bed dips to the side of me, and I feel a hand run over my head.

"Do you still want this place?" Dan asks softly. I lift my head and look around the room.

"It's my dream home," I sigh, turning my attention back

to Dan. "But how can I stay here when I never feel safe? The thought of being here on my own terrifies me," I admit. Dan watches me for a moment.

"Then I will stay every night until you feel safe again. I will not stop until I stop the guy. I already have a good idea who it is."

"Who?" I demand as Dan catches himself. He rubs his hand over his face.

"I don't have proof. I will know for sure when I see if the person I think it is has a tattoo on their right arm."

"It's Tim! That son of a bitch, I'll kill him," I shout, jumping off the bed and charging towards my dresser. Dan steps beside me and turns my body so I'm facing him.

"As fucking hot as it is watching you get angry, you can't kill him. We need to do this the right way; otherwise, you and I will end up in more trouble than him," he explains as I frown.

"*You* won't get into any trouble if *I* kill him?"

"Who do you think will hold the fucker down whilst you kill him?" Dan smirks as I pout and cross my arms over my chest.

"Maybe I don't need you to hold him down? I grew up with Billy and Luke, after all."

"And what do you think would happen if he managed to hurt a single hair on your head?" Dan asks as he twists a section of hair around his finger.

"I don't know," I point out, wanting to know what he will do. Dan's eyes darken as he stares deep into mine.

"I would happen, sweetheart. I would kill him with my bare hands if he lays one finger on you. Because no one touches what's mine."

When he talks like that, it turns me into a horny mess. Dan must notice as he grins as he runs his knuckles down my bare arm, and I realise I'm still naked. I glance down and see my nipples are hard and pointing straight at him with arousal.

"Do you like the idea of that? Are you mine, Lily bear?"

I wrap my arms around his neck and grin while pressing my body against his. Dan wraps an arm around my waist.

"Maybe. What are the benefits of being yours?"

"There's the protection of me being a law enforcer," Dan whispers as he kisses my shoulder. "There's the fact I can cook and clean, so you won't need to do it all on your own." He presses his lips to my neck. "There is also the guarantee that you will always find your pleasure many times before I find my own," he whispers against my lips before picking me up and carrying me over to the bed where he lies me underneath him.

"That's a guarantee, is it?" I tease. Dan smirks as he runs his hand up the inside of my leg until his finger is right there rubbing my sensitive clit.

"Let me prove it to you."

Chapter Sixteen

DAN

Facing the one-way glass, I watch a couple of my colleagues interview Tim.

I hadn't been in the office for more than a minute before pulling up his records to find out what his dad was implying yesterday. What I read was enough to trigger my memory.

Tim had been a suspect in a few cases involving women who were being stalked. They all told the same story of waking up at night to sounds from inside the house. Finding doors and windows unlocked or open, they all felt like they were being watched. The one thing that connected Tim to the cases was that all had just moved into a property they had leased or bought from Mr Gerald. It's been a few years since anyone made any complaints. We had all figured we were wrong, and it wasn't Tim. The Geralds had fired a handyman they used around the same time the complaints stopped, which made us all believe he had been the perpetrator, not Tim. Judging by everything Lily has been going through, there was no doubt in my mind this time.

"Hear you have a strong case against him." The sheriff stops beside me, watching the proceedings in the other room.

"He's who Mrs Guest has been seeing behind her place," I explain as Tim leans back in his chair, looking unfazed by everything.

"How are you so sure?"

"The other day, she found a leather glove just outside her garden; I found the other one in his car as well as a set of keys to Lily Johnson's new place." I finally turn to look at my boss who is frowning at me.

"She told me the other day that she felt like she was being watched. Last night, she found her back door open when she returned from being out for the day. I stayed on her couch to give her peace of mind. Luckily, I did as someone tried to enter the building with their own keys. They got away before I could catch them, but I did see a glimpse of a tattoo on their right arm."

The sheriff looks at Tim, who has rolled up his shirt sleeves, revealing the tattoo on his right arm.

"Did you search his room?"

"Yes, sir, I found an empty cash sack; his Pa confirmed it was from the break-in, as well as what I can only assume are drugs. I'm waiting for the lab to get back to me confirming what they are." I reply, turning back to watch through the glass.

"Do you think that's why he took the money?"

"His pa admitted he'd cut him off to all the finances a couple of weeks before the break-in due to his habit. I think the thought of Tim being behind bars and not at home was a bit of a relief for him. I wouldn't be surprised if Tim had threatened his pa to ensure he didn't report him to us."

The sheriff goes quiet as we watch and listen to all discussed in the other room. When Lily's name is mentioned, and they ask him about all that she has reported to me, I have to clench my jaw and fists to stop myself from charging in there and punching the bastard.

When we returned to Lily's house last night, I took a formal statement and filled out all of the paperwork, and I was planning on bringing it forward today. After everything that happened during the night, there was no way she wasn't pressing charges. I wouldn't have allowed her to brush it under the rug. I'd even threatened to tell her brothers as I thought she was in danger, but she quickly agreed to file the charges.

I watch the interview end and walk out of the room at the same time Tim is escorted out. As soon as he sees me, a smug smile appears.

"Deputy Thomas, I hope your Lily finds out who has been watching her. I'm sure her brothers will sleep easy knowing you are there with their little sister."

"Move along, Tim; some of us have places to be. Unlike you, can't say Christmas in a cell is very appealing," I reply with a smirk.

I watch as he is escorted back to the cells before turning to the sheriff.

"Mind if I pop off early? I have a few things I need to pick up before the shops close."

Sheriff Hobbs nods as he walks beside me, heading to the locker rooms.

"Yeah, enjoy your time off whilst you can. You've certainly earned it the last few days."

I call my thanks as I rush off to get my things together so I can buy what I need for tonight. After everything Lily has been through, I think she deserves to be spoilt and treated to a romantic, festive evening before I'm forced to leave her for a few days. Grabbing my phone, I pull up the shopping list I made earlier and head off to get everything we will need.

Chapter Seventeen

LILY

"Auntie Lily, push me higher!"

I laugh whilst grabbing the swing my brothers and Pops built in the garden for their growing collection of grandkids and swing my niece as high as I dare. She squeals, laughing, which puts an even bigger smile on my face.

"Somethings different about you?"

I look at Elli leaning against the fence beside Rachel, who has a sleeping Imogen in a baby-wearing sling.

"Me?" I ask, trying to sound innocent, but one look at my sisters tells me I'm failing.

"I think she's getting some," Rachel suggests grinning. I can feel my cheeks burning as I look away.

"Oh my god, you are!" Elli exclaims, pushing herself upright. "Who?"

"None of y'all's damn business," I reply, pushing Skyla again, looking for a distraction.

"I'm going to find out!" Elli declares as she pulls her phone out of her pocket.

"Stalk her Facebook, see if there's anything new on there," Rachel suggests as Elli chuckles.

"Yeah, because I'm stupid enough to plaster it all over social media," I sigh, shaking my head.

"Check who has started liking and commenting on her posts, El. That's a sure way to know," Rachel laughs, looking over a smirking Elli's shoulder. I panic, wondering if Dan HAS liked and commented on more pictures than usual, but then I remember I haven't been posting on there, so he can't have.

We decided to keep things quiet for a few days until Dan can speak to Luke and Billy. It will mean we spend Christmas apart, but we are both okay with that. I planned to stay with my parents from Christmas Eve until the morning after Christmas anyway. Afterwards, we will return to my place and spend a couple of days together before we face my brothers. Is it ideal? Probably not, but we aren't expecting them to take it well and don't want to cause any arguments during Christmas. I know it's for the best, but I hate the idea of spending time away from him over the festive period. Dan's on duty Christmas day anyway, as he always agrees to work it, so those with young families can have it off. He joked about wanting it off next year as we might have a kid, but I slapped his chest and told him to think again.

My phone rings out, and I answer it eagerly.

"Skyla, get Auntie Lils phone for me, and I'll make sure Santa brings you that pony!" Rachel calls as Elli laughs aloud.

"Skyla, ask Mommy how babies got into her and Auntie El's bellies," I call out whilst walking away with my phone to my ear.

"Ouch, what did Rach do to deserve that?" I hear Dan chuckle through the phone.

"Apparently, I'm too happy, so I must be getting some. She and Elli are trying to work out who with," I explain as I hear Skyla and her mom talking loudly.

"Well, you did get some. Actually, a little more than some," Dan teases playfully.

"I sure did," I reply, grinning, as I start to warm between my legs. "Were you in trouble for being late to work?"

"Nah, I told them I was checking something out. They hadn't even noticed I wasn't in. I'm leaving town now. I got a present for you," he says as I start feeling excited, knowing I will see him soon.

"For me? What is it?" I ask excitedly.

"You will have to see, won't you? Now hurry up. I will be there in less than ten minutes."

I end the call quickly before turning back to see the others watching me with big grins.

"I'm heading off. I'll see you in two days!" I call, not bothering to wait and see what they have to say in return.

"See you Christmas Eve, Auntie Lils!" I hear Skyla call. I turn around to see her waving whilst standing on the fence.

"See you then, Skyla. Save me a cookie!" I call back before rushing into the house to say bye to Ma and Pops.

I'm just climbing into my truck when my phone pings with a message.

Dan: I'm here. Drive carefully, Lily bear. Xxx

Since leaving the cabin this morning at the same time as

Dan, I've been so happy that I hadn't even thought about why I was at the ranch and not at my own home.

When Dan was finally getting ready for work this morning, he told me he didn't want me there alone until he could make sure that it is Tim who keeps trying to get in and was hoping to arrest him. He asked me to spend the day at my parents' to ensure that I was around others and safe. He also promised to cook dinner and keep me entertained, so I didn't even think about the possibility of another visit from our not-so-friendly guest. How can a girl say no to an offer like that?

Chapter Eighteen

DAN

When I hear Lily's car pull up outside, a nervous smile spreads across my face. I open the front door in time to see her hop out with a big grin.

"Look at you all smiley and waiting for me. Anyone would think you've missed me," she chuckles, walking towards me. I meet her on the porch and pull her forward, grab her ass and pick her up so she has no other option than to wrap her legs around my waist, causing her skirt to ride up, exposing her to me. As soon as I have her secure, I reach up with one hand, thread my fingers into her hair and force her head down so I can kiss her whilst carrying her into the house. Kicking the door closed, I pin her against it and ensure she can feel just how hard I am for her.

"Dan!" she gasps as my lips leave hers so I can kiss her neck.

"I need you," I moan against her skin as I let my hands wander over her backside and move her thong out of the way so I can feel her warm, plump lips. "It feels like you need me just as much," I point out as I slide one finger into her soaking wet entrance. The sound that she makes causes me to moan into her neck. I lift my head to find her leaning back into the door, her eyes closed and her mouth open slightly as she loses herself to the pleasure I'm providing. Fuck, if that doesn't make me primal, I don't know what would.

I remove my finger, causing her to moan for a whole different reason. Chuckling, I unzip my pants and finally free my restricted rock-hard cock. The things this woman does to me. Her body drives me wild, and all I can think about is being inside her.

"Dan," Lily moans as her lips find mine. Her fingers thread into the hair at the back of my head, keeping me in place.

I hold her underwear to one side and slip inside of her, losing myself in the warmth of her. She is everything I ever looked for in a partner; she was moulded and made to take me. Everything about her is my perfect counterpart, and I can't believe I've been blind for so long.

"Dan," she cries out as I start thrusting in and out of her. The feel of her makes me wild. Lily deserves flowers, chocolates and romance, and she will get all of that. But she also wants a man who will fuck her hard and love her harder, and, fuck, if I'm not willing to be all of that in one possessive package.

"I've been unable to think of anything else all day but this," I growl against her mouth. "I fucking love how you take me. How you moan when I pound this perfect pussy." Part of me wishes Tim wasn't locked up. What I'd give for him to turn up now. Let him see me fucking what he wants but will never have. I would let him watch me make her scream my name as she cums around my cock. Before I fill her with my release, claiming her and making her mine.

Then I would shoot the fucker right between the eyes so the last thing he ever saw was my cock buried deep in the woman he wanted but could never have because she's mine.

"Dan, harder, please."

The sound of Lily's sweet voice begging for more snaps me out of the daydream as I focus purely on her needs. I'm determined to make her scream at least once before I lose control and explode within her.

I pick up the pace as she cries out, her fingers digging into my shoulders so hard, I'm sure she would break the skin if my shirt wasn't in the way.

"Whatever you need, I'll give you," I groan through my teeth as I feel her starting to tighten around me, making it harder not to cum. I know I need to hold back just a little longer, but fuck she's too perfect.

"Can you take it, Lily bear? Can you take it all?" I ask through gritted teeth, knowing I'm about to explode.

"Yes!" she cries out as I slam a hand on the door beside her head.

"Then cum, baby girl. Cum on my dick, and make it yours," I yell as I lose it and cum hard inside her as she screams through her orgasm, contracting hard around my cock, milking me of every last drop.

For what feels like minutes, we stay there, her legs around my waist and back against the door, our heads resting on each other's shoulders as we try to catch our breaths. Three words are on the tip of my tongue, but the fear of rejection stops me from muttering them. I might have walked away from a lot of women in my time, but the thought of this woman walking away from me terrifies me to a level I never knew existed.

"Was that my surprise? Because if it was, I would like to be surprised more often, please."

I laugh as I lift my head from her shoulder and press my lips to hers, lifting her from the door and carrying her to the sofa. I place her down and reluctantly let her go so I can stand and fasten my trousers back up.

"That wasn't your surprise, although I'm more than happy to do that as often as you can take it," I wink before walking into the kitchen. "Close your eyes!" I call out before peeking around the doorframe to find her frowning at me whilst pulling her skirt down. "Close them, or I'll take the surprise back!" I warn. Lily quickly closes her eyes; I watch her momentarily to ensure she doesn't peek. I pick up a large box I hid in here before she arrived and look around the door again to check if she's still keeping her eyes closed.

"Can I look yet?" she asks as I walk back into the room.

"One minute."

I place the box on the sofa beside her and watch her confusion as she keeps her eyes shut.

"Okay, you can open them."

Lily opens her eyes and instantly looks to her right where I place the gift box. She stares at it for a moment before turning to look at me.

"I know we said no presents, and this isn't a Christmas present. It's more of a housewarming, date night present," I explain as a smile appears on her face.

"Date night? Are there rude things in here, Daniel?" That devious grin appears, and even though I just came less than five minutes ago, I can feel myself getting hard again.

"Well, now I wish there was!" I sigh dramatically as she giggles. "Just open it, already!" I laugh as nerves fill my gut. I've never done anything like this before, and I can't help wondering if I have made a huge mistake.

I watch Lily untie the bow, loosening the large tartan

ribbon before lifting off the lid. She looks inside, and the biggest smile I have ever seen spreads across her face.

"Is that?" she doesn't finish the sentence as she pulls out a pair of red tartan pyjamas, quickly followed by a second pair. "You got us matching pajamas? Please say they are matching!" she laughs as she lifts one of the pairs.

"They aren't matching as such," I declare, grabbing the set I know is mine. "But they have matching bottoms. I'm not doing matching pyjamas, no matter how happy it would make you," I roll my eyes as she giggles on the sofa before looking back into the box.

"There's all sorts in here!" she exclaims as she starts pulling out a thick Christmas throw, stuff to make mulled wine, hot chocolate, and eggnog. But when she sees the pieces at the bottom of the box, she frowns at me.

"I love the decorations, but I don't have a tree," she points out. I wink before disappearing into the kitchen.

"I know that's why I picked up this for you," I call back as I walk in carrying the pine tree.

"Oh, my goodness! Dan!" I hear her exclaim as I place the tree against the front door. I turn just in time to catch her as she launches into my arms. "I can't believe you did all this!" she exclaims as she leans back so I can look into her brown eyes.

"I hope they are happy tears?" I ask, cupping her face with my hand. She nods as she lifts onto her tip toes and kisses me. "Good. Because I have a lot planned, and the only crying you will be doing is over those cheesy Hallmark movies you love so much."

Pulling my phone out of my pocket I hit play, having already connected it to her Bluetooth speakers. Christmas music fills the air as I wink, lift her hand and spin her around. "But first, I want to hold you close and enjoy the feeling of you in my arms as we dance."

Chapter Nineteen

LILY

I lie back against Dan's chest as he holds me from behind. We're sitting on the floor by the open fire, wrapped in a blanket, watching a cheesy film. The tree is up and decorated beautifully. We have strung lights from the wooden beams on the ceiling, drank all the mulled wine and started on the eggnog. I've lost count how many times he has pulled me into his arms and danced with me. Resting my head against his shoulder as he leads, feels so wonderful and special. Dancing with Dan may be one of my favourite ways to spend my time.

I still can't believe this is the man who has driven me mad with my brothers all these years. It's as if we were waiting for the right moment to become one. Everything about him feels right. From the way he texts me when he isn't around to the way we come together sexually. It feels like he was made to be a part of me, and even after only a few short days, I can't help thinking I'm falling in love with him.

But even with everything being so perfect, I can't help

but wait for the bomb to drop on us. There is still the matter of Tim and how I will need to go to court about it all. Dan told me earlier that he arrested him this morning for the robbery at his dad's business and for stalking me. He expects him to be in over Christmas, which takes some of the worry away.

But then we have the problem of telling my family. I know my brothers are going to kill Dan; he's not known for having steady relationships. I'm not a fool. I know about his reputation and how much he has slept around, and right now, that worries me. He says I'm different from everyone else, but that doesn't help my growing worry that I'm falling for a player.

"What's going on in that head of yours, Lily bear?" Dan asks placing his chin on my shoulder. "Are you okay?"

I nod as I lean into him, not wanting to burst the bubble we have found ourselves in tonight.

"Why don't I believe you? What's going on?"

I take a deep breath and turn to kneeling in front of him. Dan sits up straighter, looking concerned.

"Do you really believe that it's all over with Tim? That he won't get out and try to get in here again?"

"It's over, baby. I even made sure I knew it was him. He knows it won't be a warning shot next time." Dan cups my cheek with his hand. "I won't have you scared in your own home. If this is your dream home, then hopefully, you will want it to be *our* home one day, but for now, I will settle for you being safe when I'm not here."

I close my eyes and lean into his hand. Taking a deep breath, I know I need to ask the big question, but I don't want to ruin everything

"Are you like this with other women?"

"Is that what's worrying you?"

I open my eyes to see Dan watching me. His head tipped slightly to the side as he ran his thumb over my cheek. I nod as he lets out a deep sigh.

"No, Lily bear. I've never been like this with anyone else." Dan lets go of my cheek and runs his fingers through his hair.

"Whilst you were sitting there worrying that I was playing you, I was here thinking how stupid I've been, never realising what I was looking for was right in front of me the whole time." He moves so he's kneeling in front of me. He takes my hands and presses a kiss to my knuckles. "I've been thinking about what we could do differently next year and if we should get more lights. Nothing about this is normal, but it feels so right." He leans in and kisses me just as his phone starts to ring. He sits back and sighs before reaching over for it.

"I'm off duty for another twelve hours," he sighs down the phone before I watch his whole-body language change. His back stiffens, and his eyes snap to mine. "What do you mean he made bail?"

I instinctively reach out for him as fear crashes into my stomach. Dan holds my hand as he listens to whoever is on the phone.

"Fuck. I can already guess who he called," Dan curses as I hear a truck coming up the drive and screeching to a stop outside. Dan ends the call and pulls me to my feet. "Go upstairs, and whatever you hear, don't come out."

The front door flies open to reveal Luke and Billy standing there. Both of them are pumped up and looking furious.

"You fucking arsehole!" Luke flies into the room towards Dan, who grabs me and moves me out of the way before putting his hands up.

"Luke, buddy. Stop."

Luke's fist makes contact with Dan's face, and I scream as I throw my hands over my mouth. I shout for Luke to stop, but Billy grabs my arm and holds me back.

"Get upstairs; I'll deal with you in a minute!" Billy snaps, pointing towards the stairs.

"No! This is my house!" I shout as he stares at Dan, who is bleeding from his nose. I pull my arm from Billy's grasp and step towards Dan. But this time, Luke steps in front of me and stands between me and Dan. Luke's attention is on his friend, who wipes the blood from his face.

"Been a while since you managed to draw blood," Dan chuckles as he looks down at his now bloody hand. "Take it, Tim called you," he adds as he looks at his best friend.

"How long have you been fucking my baby sister?" Luke yells as he steps forward. I jump around him and put myself between him and Dan.

"Luke, stop! You can't come in here throwing fists just because of me being with a guy," I start, but Luke glares at me.

"He is using you like he's used every woman in this town!" Luke snaps before looking at his friend. "What was it? You ran out of others to fuck, so you moved on to the younger ones?"

"It's not like that!" I protest, but Luke grabs my arm and pulls me roughly away from Dan.

"Get your fucking hands off her, Johnson!" Dan snarls behind me. Luke looks up at him with wide eyes.

"Don't tell me what to do with my sister. You have no say in anything regarding her," Luke snaps. Dan steps forward, purely focused on my brother's hand.

"I do when you are hurting her. Let Lily go, now!"

Luke drops my arm, and I instantly move to Dan's side.

"Now, can we talk about this like adults and not kids on the playground?" I snap, looking at my two brothers.

"Lily, you don't know what he's like," Billy starts, staring at Dan.

"Oh, don't come in here trying to defend my honour and innocence that passed a long time ago." Both of the guys snap their heads in my direction, and I swear I hear Dan chuckle behind me.

"Lils, he uses girls and dumps them without any consideration for them. I will not let him do that to you!" Luke yells, pointing angrily at Dan.

"And what if it's the other way round, and I'm using him to keep people like Tim away? Did you ever consider that?" I demand.

"Are you?" all three guys ask together. I roll my eyes and turn to Dan.

"No, you moron."

He smirks as I turn back to my brothers staring at Dan.

"Look, we were going to talk to you after Christmas," Dan starts, but Luke bursts out laughing.

"Now I know you're lying, you son of a bitch! Because how can you talk to us when you won't even be here!"

"What?" I ask, frowning. I look to Billy, who nods at me.

"It's true, Lil. He's got a new job out of state and is transferring in January."

I feel like someone pulled the rug from out from underneath me.

"Lily bear, I was going to tell you."

I turn around and stare at him. He looks paler than he did a moment ago. He opens his mouth to say something, but nothing comes out.

"It's true?" I ask as my throat closes and my eyes burn.

"No, well, yes, but."

"Don't try and talk your way out of this. You are leaving because you are bored with your life here and want something more interesting than dealing with animal callouts. Isn't that the reason you gave your boss?" Luke snaps behind me. I watch Dan as he doesn't take his eyes off mine.

"Yes, but that was before."

I hold up my hand to stop him. I can't listen to his excuses right now.

"Go, Dan."

The words hardly leave my mouth as I try desperately to keep it together.

"Lily bear I - "

I don't let him finish; I turn, walk away, and head up the stairs.

I can hear him calling my name, followed by him and Luke shouting at each other at the same time. I can't focus on who is shouting what, and don't try. I walk into my room and close the door behind me before falling to the floor and crying as my heart breaks.

Chapter Twenty

DAN

I lift my phone and check for any messages but there's nothing. It's been nearly forty hours since the Johnson brothers forced me out of Lily's house. I tried to make them see the truth, but they wouldn't listen. They wouldn't let me see or speak to her. I wouldn't even know where she was if Elli hadn't texted to say she was at the ranch and she would be safe.

While arguing with her brothers, I told them everything about Tim breaking into the place and trying to scare her. They wouldn't look at it as if I was trying to protect her; all they could see was that I had used her. But they could not be more wrong.

"Merry Christmas, Deputy Thomas!"

I look up from the quiet phone to see the sheriff walking in with a plate of food.

"Present from the wife. She told me to send her love and thanks for working today."

Every year, he brings me a plate of his wife's Christmas

dinner. It's the best part of working through Christmas. But today, I can't face it. Instead, I nod and watch as he places it before me.

"Want to talk about it?" he asks, leaning back against the desk. I flick the top of my pen and shake my head.

"Nothing to say."

"Well, that's the biggest pile of shit I've ever heard come out of your mouth, son."

I look up at him and see he has a lot to say, and I won't have a choice but to listen.

"What are you doing here, Dan?"

I look around the office and shrug.

"Working," I reply sarcastically, earning me an eye roll.

"I have watched you grow from a skinny stick of a boy who would be blown over in a strong breeze to an officer of the law who is respected by nearly every person in this town and the surrounding ones. For crying out loud, I've spent more time with you than I have my own kids over the years," he declares. I look up at him as I let out a deep sigh.

"What's your point?" I ask, wanting the lecture over so I can go back to sulking in peace.

"My point is that you have been different the last few weeks, and it's all thanks to that Johnson girl. You have laughed, smiled and seemed genuinely happy to be here. I also know about your phone call to the sheriff in Georgia three days ago. So I'm going to ask again. What are you doing here?"

I look up at him and bite back another sarcastic remark.

"She doesn't want to know." I look at my phone, which is silent.

"Have you called her?" the sheriff asks.

"Yes."

"More than once?"

I look away and shake my head. I know if she didn't pick up the first time, she wouldn't pick up any others.

"Have you at least let her know what you decided?"

I shrug my shoulders and watch my phone as if it will make her call or message me.

"I want to! I want to go round there and demand she speaks to me. That she listens and believes I was going to tell her everything. But she won't listen; if she did, her brothers would ensure she didn't get to. They told me under no uncertain terms what would happen if I tried to contact or see her again." I lean back in my chair and rub my face with my hands. "Why did the one woman who made me feel something for the first time in years have to be the one I couldn't have?"

We sit silently for a moment as I wait for him to tell me that the guys were right when they told me I wasn't good enough for her. That Lily would never trust me after I hid the truth from her. They wouldn't give me a chance to explain, and I don't think they ever will.

"Have you quite finished with the pity party for one?"

I stop staring at the ceiling and look at my boss as he watches me.

"When have you ever let people tell you what you can and cannot do? When I told you you'd never have what it takes to make it through the academy what did you do?" he demands as I stare at him. He rolls his eyes as he shakes his head in dismay. "You came out top of the class and said you had to prove me wrong. When you went into your first murder scene, and they were taking bets on how long it would take you to empty your guts, what did you do?"

"I held it until they were gone and then puked until I brought up blood," I point out.

"But you still refused to back down to them and were determined to prove yourself. So back to my original question, what the fuck are you doing here?"

Chapter Twenty-One

LILY

I smile when people talk to me or feel them watching, but inside, I'm broken. Why the hell didn't I give him a chance to explain? Surely, if he were leaving in the new year, he wouldn't have been saying everything he did, like how he wanted to have more lights up next year and the cabin eventually becoming our home. But then I think of everything the guys told me when he left. About how he was a player and how he has been complaining about being bored and wanting a new challenge. They really believe that I was that challenge, and it's hard to argue with that logic, even if it feels wrong.

"Lily dear, you're very quiet. Is everything okay?" Ma asks as she sits down next to me. I force another smile as I nod, not trusting my voice enough to speak. The guys had told me not to tell Ma and Pops about everything, as they didn't think it was fair to ruin Christmas. But looking at Ma now, I want to break down and tell her everything. I notice she still has her apron on from cooking dinner. She reaches into the front pocket and pulls out a small gift box.

"Has this got something to do with why you look so heartbroken?" she places it in my hand, and I look down at the tag.

Merry Christmas, Lily bear.
Yours always
Dan. Xxx

"I found it on the front porch this morning when I went to get the eggs from the chickens whilst everyone was sleeping. I meant to give it to you before but figured you didn't want your brothers to know."

"It's complicated, Ma," I sigh as I look at the box. I lift the lid and see a small note inside. I lift the note and spot a beautiful necklace with a bear holding a flower charm. It's childish and cute, and I love it.

"I'll leave you to read whatever that is in peace. But just remember, your happiness matters as much to me as your brothers'. That doesn't mean I will stand by and watch you throw away something that makes you happy because of them." With that, she presses a kiss on my head and stands up. Leaving me on my own to read the note.

Lily bear,
I know we said no presents, but I saw this and thought of you immediately. It's nothing special, and I know you will probably never wear it, but I had to give it to you.
I wish with all my heart things were different. I wish I had told you the truth because then, maybe you wouldn't hate me.
I turned down the position. I can't leave you without seeing where this could go with us. You make me feel things I never thought I would feel. I want to give you everything you could ever possibly need because you are the most important thing in my life. I can't believe it took me so long

to realise everything I had been looking for was right in front of me the whole time.

The tears stream down my face silently as I read his confession, and my heart breaks all over again. How had I been so blind and foolish?

"Do you want me to break your jaw this time? Cause I fucking will!"

My head snaps up as I hear Luke shout from the other room.

"Luke, enough!" Elli hisses through her teeth.

"I just want to speak to her. Let me tell her the truth, and then let her decide." I hear his voice and rush from the window seat I've been hiding on most of the day.

"You are saying nothing! I won't let you hurt her any more than you already have," Billy warns. I walk into the hallway to see my two brothers, their wives and Dan standing in the doorway in his police uniform. As soon as Dan's eyes find mine, I see the pain in them.

"Is this true?" I ask, holding up the letter. "Is this the *honest* truth?"

"I meant every word, Lily bear."

I go to take a step forward at the same time as Luke grabs hold of Dan's shirt.

"What the hell is all this noise? Luke, put Dan down this instant!"

We all turn to see Ma and Pops walking into the hallway.

"Does someone want to tell me what the hell is going on?" Pops demands.

"Sir, I'm in love with your daughter."

All heads snap to face Dan, who stands tall and proud as he looks at my father.

"I know it's not what Luke, Billy and probably yourself want to hear, but it's the truth." He turns to look at me and gives me that soft smile that makes butterflies erupt in my stomach. "I meant every word in that letter. I hadn't told you about the job because there was nothing to tell. I turned it down a few days before things even started getting serious because the thought of leaving you behind didn't feel right."

"Oh please," Luke sighs as he crosses his arms over his chest.

"Luke, will you shut up? This has nothing to do with you," Ma snaps at my brother.

"It has everything to do with me. She is my sister, and he -"

"Is your best friend and has stood by you through thick and thin. Now give it a break." Ma turns to me and winks before I hear Pop clearing his throat.

"Your mother's right." He turns his focus to me. "How do you feel about Dan, sweetheart?"

I look back at Dan and smile.

"I love him too."

"Then I don't see what the problem is." Pop turns back to Luke and Billy. "If he hurts her, then you can kill him and bury his body in the top field. Otherwise, get out of the way and give them some space."

I hear Luke and Billy say something, but all I can see is Dan as I run to him and throw my arms around his neck.

"I'm so sorry, Lily bear. I swear I was going to tell you everything once my boss knew I wasn't leaving. I don't even know how Tim found out," he sighs into my neck. I lean back so I can see him.

"He overheard two guys talking about it at the station." I watch as Dan closes his eyes and kisses my forehead whilst sighing.

I can still hear Luke and Billy arguing with Pops, so I take Dan's hand and lead him out of the front door and onto the porch, where I sit on the porch swing. He sits beside me so I can lean into him.

"Did you mean what you said about next Christmas? About still wanting us to be together?"

"I told you; I meant every word. You mean so much to me, baby girl. I will never hide anything from you again. You have my word on that."

I lean in and press a kiss to his lips.

"I believe you."

The front door opens, and Elli and Rach come out.

"Well, talk about family drama at Christmas," Rachel sighs as Elli laughs. Dan jumps to his feet and signals for her to sit down.

"Thanks," she smiles as she sits next to me.

"So now the cat's out of the bag; Pops has demanded that the guys get off their high horse and leave you two be." She turns her attention to Dan and smiles. "He has promised to help hide your body if you fuck up, so keep that in mind."

"Oh, trust me, I don't plan on fucking this up," he tells her before looking back to me grinning. We all turn as Dan's back goes ridged, and the rest of the family comes out. Skyla runs straight to her mom, who gives us all a warning look.

"Dan, I know my sons have been a little overprotective over their sister, and I understand why from what they have told me. But you said you love our Lily, and I believe you. So, if either of her brothers gives you a hard time again, I would like you to tell me, and I will make sure they leave you both in peace."

I stand from my seat and hug Pops before looking over

his shoulder and sticking my tongue out at my two frowning brothers.

"He still stands by. We can kill him if he hurts you," Billy says, glaring at Dan.

"I will hand myself over if I ever do," Dan replies, and I roll my eyes.

"Then enough of all this; it's Christmas, and I insist that Dan joins us for the rest of the day," Ma announces, smiling as she threads her arm through mine.

"Actually, ma'am, I need to get back to work. Mrs Hobbs would never make me another Christmas dinner if her husband has to cover me for more than an hour," Daniel explains with a smile.

"Well then, we insist you take some food with you. Let me go and plate you up some bits, and don't even try to argue with me." She turns on her heels and marches into the house, no doubt to pile as much food as she can on to the biggest plate she can find.

"Ma! Don't be giving him all my mince pies! Cowboy, stop her!" Elli yells, trying to climb to her feet, but she can't manage it as quickly as she would like. Luke sighs as he turns to Dan.

"Can you help her up? I'll save the fuuffffreaking pies," he glances at Skyla, who is glaring at him because she knows what he was about to say. "I didn't say it!" he declares before walking into the house and calling out to Ma.

Dan steps forward and helps Elli get to her feet.

"Thanks. I'll be so glad when this baby is out." She runs her hand over her bump and holds out her hand for Skyla. "Come on, pudding thief; I need some pies and cookies stolen." She looks over her shoulder and winks at the two of us before heading into the house followed by

Rach and Billy, who nods once at Dan and me before leaving.

"I have a feeling I'm going to be enemy number one for a while with them," Dan sighs as he rubs his face. I walk up to him and wrap my arms around his waist as he places an arm around my shoulder.

"You sure she's worth the hassle?" Pops asks as I gasp, and Dan laughs before pressing a kiss to the hair on the top of my head.

"She sure is, sir."

Pop nods at us before turning around and heading towards the door.

"I'll leave you two in peace before you head back to work." He stops at the door and looks at me with a smile. "Hopefully, you will now enjoy Christmas a little more than you have been, Lils."

"I will, Pops," I reply as I feel Dan's arms tighten around me. "Thank you for sticking up for us," I add. Pops looks at me for a moment and smiles.

"You will always be my baby, Lily May, but I know I need to accept you are a grown woman and sensible enough to make your own decisions, even if I don't always like them. But I do know I will rest easier knowing you have Dan with you out in those woods."

"You have my word. I will always keep her safe," Dan answers next to me as he steps forward with his hand out. Pops takes it, and as they shake, I don't miss how he squeezes Dan's hand a little harder than necessary.

"Merry Christmas, Deputy Thomas," Pop says as he walks to the front door.

"Merry Christmas, Mr Johnson," Dan replies as we watch the front door close, finally leaving the two of us alone. Dan turns and pulls me into his arms before kissing me. I melt into his arms and kiss him back, finally letting go of all the worry and sadness that has consumed me since I last saw him.

"I need to get back to work. Can I come and see you tomorrow as planned?" he asks as I wrap my arms around his neck and smile up at him.

"You better; I need to thank you for my present," I lift on my tiptoes so my lips are by his ear. "I can think of a few ways you might enjoy. Can you bring your handcuffs home?"

Dan's lips crash into mine, taking my breath away as he kisses me passionately.

"Baby girl, I want to see you in nothing *but* my cuffs," he growls against my lips before kissing me again.

"Uh, hum."

We both turn our heads to find Grams standing behind us, holding out a platter covered in foil.

"Deputy Thomas, I believe this is for you," she says, holding out the plate.

"Thanks," Dan answers nervously as I bury my face in his chest, giggling nervously. I step back as Dan takes the platter from Grams, who winks at him as he does. "Please thank Mrs Johnson for me; I'm sure I will enjoy all of this," he stammers before turning back to me. "See you tomorrow at one?" he asks, his cheeks bright red.

"She'll be there with bells on … or should that be cuffs?"

"Grams!" I laugh as Dan chokes and rushes towards the police cruiser, which is parked in front of the house.

"See you later, Lily Bear," he calls, placing the platter on the back seat before opening the driver's door and looking back at me. He stares at me for a moment with a soft smile on his face. "I love you." I don't stop to think as I rush down to him and jump into his arms, kissing him again.

"I love you too," I whisper, smiling as I step back.

"See you tomorrow," he says, running his knuckles down my cheek.

"See you at home," I reply, grinning as I step back and watch him climb into the car.

I wave as he turns around and heads off back towards town, where the police station is.

"You know, I always liked him," Grams smiles as I walk back up towards the front door, which Grams holds open.

"I like him too," I reply, linking my arm with hers as we walk into the house, and I know the whole day will feel much better now that I have my man back.

Chapter Twenty-Two

DAN

I hear the front door open as I shove some stuff in my overnight bag.

"Dan?" Mitch calls out. I stop and, for a moment, wonder if he is here to kill me for the Johnson brothers.

"Yeah," I call back, picking up my bag and walking into the lounge of my apartment, where I see Mitch standing with his arms crossed over his chest. He looks down at the bag in my hand and sighs.

"So, it's true then? You and Lils?"

"Yep. I take it Luke called you," I sigh, placing the bag by the front door and heading into the open-plan kitchen.

"Billy. I think he was hoping I would kill you for him as his old man has told him he has to leave you alone."

I laugh as I pour myself a glass of water and turn back to Mitch while sipping it.

"Sounds about right. Go ahead, get it off your chest. I have spent the last two days at work and want to be at Lily's by the time she arrives from her parents." I finish my drink and place the glass in the sink. Looking back at Mitch, I find him watching me, still standing there like a security guard outside a bar on a weekend.

"You care about her?" he asks.

"I love her. Cliche, I know, but she makes me feel happier than I have felt in years. Like there is nothing more important than her and her happiness."

Mitch and I stare at each other for a moment before he lets out a deep breath and nods once before turning towards the front door.

"That it? No beating or warning?" I call, stepping towards him. Mitch turns back around and looks at me.

"There is nothing that needs to be said. Like I've said, I know you better than you know yourself and believe that you love her. Old man Johnson told you what would happen if you hurt her, and I will help the brothers kill you if you do. But I don't think you will. I believe you will do anything to give her the life and love she deserves, and I, for one, am happy for you."

"Wow, that's deep, even for you," I reply as I approach him. "It's all true but deep." I smile as I look to the one friend who has always had my back. Luke and Billy have both disappeared at one time or another to do their own thing, but Mitch has never left my side.

"Well, one of us has to be deep. You've spent too long thinking with your dick for it to be you," he grins, causing me to laugh aloud.

"Fair enough, I can't argue with that." The grin from my face drops, and I look at him deep in the eye. "But those days are over for me. I will give Lily everything she needs and more. There isn't anything I'm not willing to do to keep her safe and happy."

Mitch watches me momentarily before nodding and turning back to the door.

"As long as you still make it to game night next week. Now you have a woman doesn't give you an excuse to miss it!" he calls as he walks out of the front door.

"Isn't it too soon for me to be anywhere near the Johnson brothers?" I call back, suddenly fearing for my life.

"It will be more dangerous for you to miss it, so make sure you are there!" he calls, closing the door behind him.

Shit, so much for my plan of avoiding them for a few weeks to ensure they have time to calm down and come to terms with me dating their sister.

My phone pings in my pocket, and I pull it out to a message from Lily.

Lily Bear: I'm leaving here in ten minutes. I'll be at home waiting for you and your cuffs. xxx

A winking face at the end of the message causes my cock to spring to life. Fuck it, at least I will die a happy man knowing the woman I love loves me back, and I will have had a couple of weeks loving her in every way possible before my untimely death.

Dan: On my way, I can't wait to get you all to myself finally. I love you xxx

Epilogue

LILY

Driving down the dirt road home, I let out a long, exhausted sigh. All I want to do is fall into bed with Dan and sleep for a month.

I have no idea what she did, but since Elli revamped my website three months ago, my calendar has blown up. Other than two weeks over Christmas and New Year, I haven't had an entire weekend off in months. I've been hired for weddings, christenings and parties. When Dan realised I had nothing booked for next weekend, he insisted I keep it that way, promising me a long weekend for the two of us—no work, family or friends. Just us in the cabin, ignoring the outside world for a whole four days. How's a girl meant to turn down an offer like that when she knows it will also include a lot of hot sex?

I spent today as the photographer at a wedding. Is there anything more romantic than getting married on Valentine's Day? I doubt it. The whole day was perfect, and the couple looked so happy that I couldn't help imagining my own wedding. It's something I find myself doing more often these days. I've never thought about marriage before; I was never in a serious enough relationship to consider the long-term things until now. Since Christmas, it's all I can think about. It probably doesn't help that Dan constantly talks about us and the future.

A month ago, I asked Dan to move in with me. He stayed every night he had off, so it seemed pointless for him to pay rent on an apartment he was never in. Today was officially the last day of his lease, and he would hand his keys in on his lunch break. I'd hoped to speak to him at some point, but I don't think I had more than a few seconds to myself. He was working all day today anyway and told me this morning that he wouldn't be home until late.

I glance at the time on my dashboard and see it's just gone ten PM. Dan was hoping to finish by nine-thirty, so he might not even be home yet. He rarely gets home on time when he works the late shift. That doesn't stop me from feeling disappointed when I stop outside the house and see it's pitch-black inside and his truck missing.

I turn off the engine and quickly retrieve my belongings from the back seat before heading towards the house. With my arms full, I clumsily unlock the door and rush inside to turn off the alarm. Dan insisted it was installed between Christmas and New Year. After everything that happened with Tim, he wants to ensure I never come back to an unsafe house again. The fact that he installed it with Pops and Billy may have helped start the forgiving process between them. Things still aren't perfect between him and my brothers, but they've accepted our relationship the best they could, and they no longer threaten to kill him daily. I think the fact that we were still together almost three months down the line has helped. As well as him moving in which was something he said he would never do with a girl.

Turning on the lights, I drop my camera and bag onto the chair but find myself freezing as something catches my attention.

Along the dark wooden floor are pink and white rose petals. Following the trail with my eyes, I find it leads towards the stairs and up them. I have to stop myself from squealing out loud with excitement as I rush to the stairs and follow the trail to the bedroom.

Pushing the door open, I find the room lit with a ton of candles. Petals are on the floor leading to the bed and covering the blankets. The room smells magical, but as I look around, I realise I can't see Dan anywhere. As I'm about to call out to him, two hands cover my eyes from behind.

"Surprise, Lily Bear." His voice is just a whisper in my ear as he leans in and presses a kiss to my cheek. Turning in his arms, I place mine around his neck so I can look into his warm eyes.

"I thought you were working late? Your truck's not out front."

Dan shakes his head as he pulls me against his firm body.

"Mrs Guest let me park down her place to surprise you; I couldn't resist." He presses a hard kiss to my lips before extracting himself from my arms and spinning me around before holding me close again. He pulls something from his pocket, and music fills the quiet house. He leads us into a soft dance in time to the music as I lean against his chest and let out a contented sigh.

Since the first time we danced together, Dan has ensured it happens regularly. For a man who never had a serious relationship, he pulls out all the stops when it comes to me. I've had a few jealous women approach me when out in town. Some warned that he was playing me, and others tried to scare me off as they thought he would go back to them. It's been difficult at times, and Dan thought I would leave him over it at one point, but how could I when he has been honest with me from day one? I trust the man as much as I trust my family, and now people are seeing that when it comes to Dan, the past is in the past, and as he is happy to tell anyone who will listen, I am very much his future.

"For a man who claimed to have no idea how to be romantic, you are doing a grand job," I point out, smiling to myself. Dan kisses the top of my head, which always makes my heart melt.

"I once told myself you deserved flowers, chocolates and romance, and I would ensure you got all of that."

Looking up from his chest, I fall even more in love with the man holding me. No one has ever made me feel as special and loved as he has, and I never want this feeling to end. However, I also know how this man's mind works.

"Was it just romantic things you decided I deserved, or was there something else?"

A grin spreads across Dan's face as he picks me up in one swift move and carries me over to the bed. He throws me on it and climbs between my legs, grabbing my hands and holding them against the mattress above my head.

"I also knew you'd want a man who will fuck you hard and love her harder, and judging by the way you are staring at me now with those beautiful fuck me eyes; I think I was right."

My throat seizes up, leaving me unable to speak. When he talks to me like that, I'm putty in his hands, and he knows it. Dan grinds against me, proving how desperate I am for him, and he's ready to give me anything I want.

"Fuck me, Dan," I gasp as he does it again.

"My pleasure, baby." He buries his face against my neck, kissing me in that sensitive spot that makes me weak. I try to pull my hands from his grasp, but he looks down at me with a devious grin.

"Do I need to get my cuffs? Or are you going to be a good girl and let me eat you until you scream my name and cum on my tongue?"

Holy cow, I want that. I need that more than I need the air that's not quite filling my lungs. I nod as I stare at Dan, desperate to feel him. His grin widens as his lips move, brushing lightly across mine.

"Just as I thought. Now, stay perfectly still; I want to kiss every inch of your body before getting to the best bit."

Luckily, I always wear dresses when photographing weddings, so I blend in with the guests. This one, in particular, buttons down the front, which Dan undoes in record time before making good on his promise to kiss every part of me.

His fingers slide my underwear to the side as his tongue gently brush against my clit.

"Dan," I gasp as my body comes alive.

"That's it, baby, call my name."

I open my legs further as his tongue slowly brings me to a withering mess; his grip on my hips tightens, holding me in place as he begins to feast on me.

"Dan, oh my god!" I cry out, throwing my arms over my eyes as I fall apart underneath him. He continues to lick and suck my clit until I'm begging for a rest.

Dan gently tugs my arms away from my face to reveal him smiling down at me. He's lying on top of me completely naked, and I feel the tip of him at my entrance teasing me, so I almost beg for more.

Slowly he eases himself into me, filling me to the point I almost cum from the feeling of him alone.

"You were made to be mine, baby. No one else will ever get to experience the feeling of you cuming on their cock again," he declares, grinding his hips and hitting every spot inside of me. "Every part of you was moulded for me, and no one can tell me otherwise."

Lifting my legs and draping them over his shoulders, he starts fucking me just as I asked him to. I've always liked sex, but with Dan, he fucks me or makes love to me in a way I never experienced before. He often tells me I was made for him, and there is no denying it. Everything about him is my perfect counterpart. Nothing could have prepared me for my love for the man I have known my whole life yet never truly saw until three months ago.

I don't know how long he blows my mind as he takes me over and over again—giving me orgasm after orgasm until I can barely see. He once promised I would always find my release before him, and he has never gone back on his word.

"Fuck, I love the way your body reacts to me," he moans as I know he's approaching his release. "Who do you belong to, baby?"

"You. Only ever you!" I cry out as he picks up the pace further.

"Too fucking right. You will always be mine!"

For the next few minutes, it's wild, uncensored and rough, and so fucking perfect. Dan manages to bring me to another orgasm as he finds his release, and we cum together, perfectly timed and crying out each other's names.

Dan falls to the side of me and instantly pulls me into his arms. He tightens his hold and doesn't let go while we try to catch our breath. As always, he holds me tight and peppers my forehead with kisses. For a rough lover, he is extremely loving afterwards.

"I love you." The words are barely a whisper, but my heart reacts the same whether he's declaring it to the world or just me. I don't think I could ever get tired of hearing him say those three words.

"I love you too," I reply, lifting my head to kiss him. Dan's eyes find mine, and I get lost in them. When it's just me and him like this, everything else ceases to exist. It's just me and him in our little bubble, and nothing else matters.

My phone rings out from downstairs, and for a moment, I'm about to let it ring out when I realise it's a designated ringtone.

"Shit." I jump out of bed and rush down the stairs, nearly falling over as I run to reach it before the call ends.

"I'm here! What's happened?" I demand, answering as I turn to see Dan standing behind me, completely naked, holding out his shirt for me to put on.

"I'm not going to ask what you were doing for you to take so long answering," Luke sighs down the phone.

"It's Valentine's Day. What do you think I was doing?" I point out, grinning. Luke calls out that there's too much information at the same time as Dan roars, laughing. "Why are you calling anyway?"

"I thought you wanted me to call as soon as there were any signs?"

My eyes bulge as I look at Dan, who's grinning.

"Elli's going into labour?"

"No," Luke laughs. "He's already here."

"He? She's had it? It's a boy?" I ask as tears fill my eyes.

"I don't know how I feel about you calling my son an "it", but yep. He came out kicking up a storm." I can hear the pride in my brother's voice, and I'd give my left arm that he's cried at some point.

"How's Elli? Why didn't you call me when she went into labour?"

"We didn't have time. Turns out she's been having contractions all day and thought they were just back ache as they didn't hurt that much. Ma only just made it to our house before he was born in the lounge. It all happened so quickly."

"Oh my god, but they are okay?" I ask, leaning against Dan.

"They are both amazing. The midwife just left. Mama and baby are both perfect." Again, I can hear the pride in his voice, which causes my heart to swell.

"Does he have a name?"

"William Peter Johnson. Peter after Elli's dad and Billy gave his consent to us using William as I had a boy first."

It's a tradition in our family that the eldest boy gets the name William. This tradition goes back about eight generations. Billy's birth name is William, but from a young age, Luke, Mitch, and Dan called him Billy, and it's stuck.

"I love it. Give them both a hug and a kiss from me, and let me know as soon as they are up for a visit. Aunty Lily needs cuddles," I giggle excitedly.

"Will do. Make sure Dan comes with you. He needs to meet his nephew, too." Luke hangs up before I can reply. I look up to find Dan staring at me with his mouth hanging open.

Luke and Dan's relationship hasn't been great since everyone found out about us. Even though they are pleasant to each other, Luke has kept his best friend at a distance. Which Dan has struggled with. He misses his best friend but knows he needs time to accept everything. It's evident from Dan's face that he genuinely feels blessed after Luke referred to him as little William's uncle. Dan was sure Luke would push him away further when the baby was born, but instead, he finally accepted our relationship and seemed to want his best friend back.

"I knew he would come around," I smile as Dan continues to look amazed. Placing my arms over his shoulders, I lift onto my tiptoes and kiss his lips. "It looks like you are officially a member of the Johnson family. Hope you know that means your plans now have to include my large crew."

Dan looks at me for a moment before grabbing my ass and lifting me so I can wrap my legs around his waist. Rushing up the stairs, taking them two at a time in his haste to get to where he wants us to be.

"What are you doing?" I laugh as he storms into our room, throws me back on the bed, and lies in between my legs again.

"I have big plans for us, Lily Bear. As much as our families will be a part of them, I can't wait to watch our own little family start to grow. But until then," he starts before pressing a kiss to my neck. "We are going to have a lot of fun in every room in this house until you are ready to become Mrs Thomas and a mama yourself." Dan's mouth starts making its way all over my body again as my heart fills with excitement.

"I don't want to wait too long," I gasp as he takes my nipple between his teeth.

"Oh, you won't because I want to put my ring on your finger and baby in your belly so everyone knows you belong to me."

As he takes my nipple back between his teeth, I know one thing for certain. There will never be any doubt I belong to Dan, as he belongs to me, and no one or nothing will ever come between us again.

Also by D.E. Bartley

vinci-books.com/preciouslittlerose

He bought her sanctuary. Now he wants her.

When billionaire Adam Xander sets his sights on Isabelle's cherished library—and on her—she'll have to fight harder than ever. But in a dangerous game of power, obsession, and desire, losing might mean surrendering everything.

Turn the page for a free preview…

Precious Little Rose: Prologue

"Please, sir. I swear it was only one bottle. I will pay you back, work for free; do anything!"

The pathetic prick's begging is getting on my last nerve. Looking to the side, I roll my eyes at my head of security, Vincent.

"Why are they always sorry after they've been caught?"

"Because they were caught, no other reason," he shrugs as the thief sniffs from the seat he's tied to. I turn my attention back to him as my hands curl into fists.

"Here's the thing, Chad. I know it wasn't just one bottle. If it were, I would have stopped after breaking each of your fingers. But I didn't."

"Nope, I'd say you broke at least four ribs, too," Vincent adds whimsically.

"It was, I swear! I wouldn't steal anything else from you!" The fact the guy is still trying to deny all his wrongdoings is really starting to piss me off.

"If there is anything I hate more than a thief, it's druggies and liars." Swinging my fist, I punch him in the jaw hard enough to hear it crack. Blood dribbles from his mouth as he cries out in pain. "Try lying with a broken jaw, I dare you." Watching him cry, I know each tear and sob will be adding to his pain. The way his shoulders have sagged tells me he's done. I've physically and mentally exhausted him, and there is nowhere left for him to go, and he knows it.

"Where's the money, Chad?" I demand giving him one last chance to come clean.

"I don't have it," the words barely audible, confirming I did, in fact, break his jaw.

"Then you see, we have a problem. I want my money and won't stop until I have it." I make a show of pulling my hand back, ready to punch him again.

"Stop, wait, I'll tell you." He tries to yell with his jaw hanging slightly on one side. He attempts to speak, but the pain is obviously unbearable. I should probably feel bad about that, but I don't.

"Did you get a word of that?" I ask Vincent, who sighs before pushing himself away from the wall he's leaning against.

"Why do you always break their jaw *before* they confess? It makes things so much harder." Coming to a stop in front of Chad's chair, he takes hold of the hair at the top of his head and pulls so he has no choice but to look at Vincent. "Say that again, but slower." This time, it's clearer, and I know he used the money he stole from me to buy drugs.

"Get the name of the dealer. We will pay him a visit tonight!" I snap, turning on the spot and heading for the exit. I grab my jacket off the hook and shrug it on as Vincent opens the door.

"Got the address?"

He nods and pulls out his phone.

"Good. I need to grab something from the office, and we'll head off." I stop outside the door to find two more of my men standing guard. "Get rid of him," I order, nodding towards the room I've just left. "I don't care how, just get it done. Then search his property. If you find anything that belongs to me, you can bring it to my office in the morning. Understood?" Both nod and enter the room as I leave the now-screaming Chad behind.

Vincent falls into step beside me as we walk to my office, tapping away on his phone and no doubt giving my driver directions.

I hadn't planned on coming to this club tonight; I had more important places to be, but when the manager contacted me saying he had caught the person who'd been stealing, I quickly changed my plans. I like to take care of thieves myself, especially when they have gone to the trouble of stealing over five thousand pounds in cash and stock, and that's just the stuff we know about. I'm sure Chad had a lot more from me, which is why he had to pay. I enter the room and head for my desk, where I keep my phone and keys. As I move my chair out of the way, something on the CCTV display catches my eye.

There, on the screen, is a brunette dancing with some friends. There's something about the way she moves that's mesmerising. She looks so free and happy, like she doesn't have a care in the world. For the briefest moment, she looks directly at the camera as if looking straight into my soul. I can't look away from the woman—everything about her calls to me.

I scramble for the remote, but by the time I find it, I've lost her in the sea of bodies; the only thing I catch before she disappears altogether is the small tattoo on her right shoulder. The image of her and that tattoo are imprinted on my brain, where it will stay until I can find her and make her mine. I may not know her name, but I don't care because after seeing that tattoo, I know she will now and forever be my little Rose.

Precious Little Rose: Chapter One

ROSE

Sipping my coffee, I look through the small pile of books which have arrived. This is one of my favourite parts of my job as Head Librarian; I get to see the new releases as they come in and get them ready for our regulars to read.

"Anything good in the pile today?"

I turn to see my good friend and fellow librarian, Aiden, walk into view. His mop of blonde hair is looking more unkept than I'm used to seeing it. He usually keeps it fairly short. I've also noticed his bright blue eyes have lost part of their sparkle recently.

"New releases from Charlene Harris, E. L. James and Jennifer. L. Armentrout," I reply as Aiden moans dramatically.

"How many copies of James do we have? You know the women will be kicking the door down for that one."

I laugh, knowing he's right. Ever since she brought out "*Fifty Shades of Grey*," smut has exploded in the literature world. Not that there is anything wrong with reading smut; I read a lot of it myself. When you've been single as long as I have, a good book full of sex is about as much action as you get.

"Only one, so expect at least two Karens to kick off at some point." I take another sip of my drink and hear Aiden sigh again while firing up the old and very outdated computer system.

Watching one of my closest friends, I notice that he looks a little less refined than usual, and his body language is screaming exhaustion. For a guy who usually stands tall and proud, his shoulders are slumped, and he doesn't look like he's had a decent night's sleep in days.

I walk over to his desk and sit on it to look at him. Being only five foot one, my feet dangle off the floor. Aiden turns his attention to me sceptically.

"What?"

"Don't *what* me," I warn. "What's going on with you?" I stare at him whilst holding on to the edge of the desk, letting my legs swing a little.

"Nothing," he snaps, looking back to the computer.

"I'm not buying it, so try again. I let it go when you stood us up Saturday, but now I want the truth." I continue to watch as Aiden takes a deep breath, leans back in his chair and crosses his arms over his chest.

"Fine. Andrew's left me."

"What?" My back goes poker straight as I stare at him, shocked. "When?"

"Saturday, that's why I said I was busy. When I got home after work, he had packed all his stuff. He has fallen in love with a waitress at his restaurant, and they want to get married."

"But he's gay!" I declare louder than I mean to. I slam a hand over my mouth and look around to check that no one heard me.

"Well, apparently, he's *bi*. So, he's gone, and now I live alone for the first time in two years, and I hate it." Aiden's lip quivers as he looks up at me. "I really thought he was the one, Iz."

I jump off the desk to throw my arms around him. For a moment, he freezes before melting against me and hugging me back.

"I'm so sorry, Aiden. You should have said, I would have come around. Why don't you come and stay with me until you are ready to go back," I offer, pulling away from him. He closes his eyes before taking a deep breath.

"No, it's fine. I need to be a big boy and get over it."

I shake my head as I open one of the desk drawers and pull out the set of spare keys I keep here for emergencies. I lift his hand and place them on his palm.

"You know my door is always open for you. Just come round at any time."

He looks at the keys momentarily before nodding with his eyes closed. I know better than to push him, so I wait patiently for Aiden to compose himself.

"Thanks, Izzy," he replies, giving me a sad smile. I lean over and kiss his cheek.

"That's what friends are for," I wink before returning to the books that had just come in. I hear him telling me he will go through the emails in the back room for a bit, and I hold a thumb up to signal I heard as I take the trolley of returns and start wheeling them to the library's main section.

As I walk through the bookshelves, I get lost in thought. The library is my favourite place. There is nowhere else I could ever see myself working. From the faded artwork on the walls, the beautiful ceiling and the smell of books, there is nowhere a bookworm like myself would want to spend their time.

I first visited Cogsworth Library as a young child, and I've been here nearly every week since. This is my happy place, my second home, and I love everything about it.

As I place the books back on their designated shelves, I let my mind wander to the times my dad brought me here growing up. Every Saturday, without fail, Dad would bring me to pick out new books for us to read together. I enjoyed nothing more than sitting next to the fire back home and getting lost in an adventure. I make a mental note to pick a book or two out for him later today so that he has something new to keep him entertained.

"Isabelle?"

I hear someone calling me from within the shelves and quickly abandon my trolley. I regret it when I find the local Councillor, Mr Fredrick, standing by the reception desk.

"Ah, there you are, Isabelle," he greets me with a wide grin. I try desperately to hide my unease whenever I see him. He never brings good news; I know he hates this place more than most.

"Mr Fredrick, and what have we done to earn the pleasure of your presence this morning?" I ask, hoping the irritation isn't noticeable in my tone.

"Well, I was wondering if I could have a moment of your time. The thing is, there's a matter I wish to discuss with you." He tips his head to the side, looking almost sympathetic, which instantly gets my back up as my heart skips a beat. I have a strong feeling I'm not going to like whatever he's going to say, and judging by his face, he knows it, too.

Precious Little Rose: Chapter Two

BEAST

"A library? Really Adam? Do you have no shame?"

I lean back in my large leather desk chair and sigh as I turn to look at my second-in-command with one arched brow. He is leaning on my desk as if trying to intimidate me.

"Sit the fuck down, Thomas."

He instantly does as he's told but doesn't lose that irritated look on his face. I lean forward, resting my elbows against the large mahogany desk. Placing my hands together, I stare at the guy before me.

"I have a meeting with the local councillor in half an hour to tour the building. I will then decide whether it is worth renovating."

"And if it's not?"

"Then I will buy it and the building next to it and knock it down to build an apartment block. It's the perfect location as we can charge a fortune for a river view," I explain, sitting back in my chair as Thomas rubs at his face.

"People aren't going to be happy; the library is over a

hundred years old. I'm surprised it's not a listed building, especially with the clock tower," he starts, but I cut him off with a sigh.

"Do people even use libraries anymore? Isn't everything available on tablets like Kindle and Kobo or whatever they use?" I stand, pull my suit jacket off the back of my chair and shrug it on.

"A library isn't just about the books inside. It's also the heart of the community where people come together. They host all kinds of things there, from book clubs for all ages to activity days for kids during school holidays. For some, it's the only place they can go to escape reality. I beg you to reconsider," Thomas declares as he stands. I roll my eyes as I tug my shirt cuff from underneath my jacket.

"You can beg all you like; I've made up my mind. The potential profit is too high to ignore; the council is near enough giving the building and grounds away. I would be mad not to take advantage of this opportunity." I pull a large envelope from the top drawer of my desk and drop it in front of him. "That *heart of the community* is draining the council of funds on a monthly basis. No one uses it, and if they do, they aren't putting anything into it. I'm offering to take it off their hands at a reasonable price and will consider providing a garden or something else in its place. People want somewhere to meet; they can go there." I pocket my phone and head for the door as Thomas flicks through the paperwork. "I'll be back in two hours. Try to be in a better mood by the time I return," I call, walking from the office and onto the bright floor of my office building.

My assistant's desk is situated in the middle of the floor, where she and her helper work.

"Jude, I'm going to the meeting with that arsehole, Fredrick. When Helsby gets here, put him in conference room two, I'll deal with the fucker when I'm back," I snap, straightening my red tie.

"Of course, sir. Don't forget you have the developers coming at three thirty to discuss the building on Labyrinth Street," she calls out as I step into the elevator and turn to face her. I nod once as the door closes and the elevator starts to move.

I take the time to turn to the mirror and check my appearance as I do every time I'm in here. I run my fingers through my black hair and straighten my tie again. For forty-four years of age, I look fucking good. The problem is that being rich, powerful and good-looking makes you a target for every woman in the surrounding areas. Sure, I like to mess around, but who doesn't? The problem is they all want more, and they won't get it from me.

The image of the woman with the rose tattoo fills my mind like it has every time I've stopped since Saturday. I'm determined to find her, even if it's like looking for a needle in a haystack. But first, I need to buy this library and turn it into something profitable.

The elevator opens, and I see my head bodyguard waiting for me.

"Xander."

"Vincent," I reply whilst walking towards the front door of the building. Vincent is a step ahead of me, watching for any trouble. In my line of business, I've made plenty of enemies over the years, far too many to count. Most of them are looking for a way to take me out; a handful have even tried. But all they succeeded in doing was signing their own death sentence. I have no issue getting my hands dirty, even if by eliminating a threat to my business or personal life. I'm always carrying some sort of weapon, plus I train four times a week with Vincent, who was a professional fighter. I'm the deadliest weapon anyone will ever meet.

As we get out onto the busy street, Vincent stops by my car, a black Aston Martin Rapide, and holds the door open for me. I undo my jacket button as I slide in. He closes the door and climbs into the passenger seat beside my driver, Elijah. Both have worked for me for many years and have earned my utmost trust and respect.

I don't need to tell Elijah where to go; my PA will have sent them both all my plans for the day. I take my phone from my pocket and pull up the building information I attained online this morning. It's an old two-story building, not massive, but it has the potential to be converted into a club of some sort.

My business started small, an old gentleman's club my grandfather passed down to me at the age of eighteen. He showed me how to turn that one club into a whole franchise, one that was known all over the globe. Since then, I've branched out into wine bars, nightclubs, stripper bars and apartment buildings. That's just the legal side of my business. The rest has earned me a lot of enemies, and I have blood on my hands, but if you really want to earn people's respect and make money in this world, you have put your blood, sweat, and tears into earning it. This is how I've gotten to where I am today, and no one will ever be able to stop me.

"You've got a death wish; I'll give you that," Elijah laughs from the driver's seat as he stops at a red light.

"For what reason this time?" I ask, not looking up from my phone.

"The library is loved by the whole community. Whereas you, well, are not."

Vincent laughs next to him as I shake my head.

"For a community that loves the place, they never fucking use it. The place has gone to the dogs, and the council can't afford to keep up with all the repairs," I reply as I read a new email.

"You could always do it up and turn it around," Elijah continues.

"I am, by turning it into a bar," I reply, bored of this conversation.

Everyone seems to have a problem with me buying the library, but that only makes me more determined to buy it. If you don't use it, you lose it; it's that simple.

"I meant as a library. Give it a new lease of life. If it doesn't work, at least you can say you've tried," he continues. I let out a deep sigh as I look up from my phone. Vincent looks at me with a grin as Elijah glances at me through the rearview mirror.

"Do I look like I give a shit about some old books? What is the fascination with people reading all of a sudden? Everything is available electronically now or online, anyway," I point out. "If I buy the property, I will be renovating as soon as possible, and not into a fucking library," I snap. The two guys in front of me share a look before thankfully dropping the subject. I go back to reading the business news in peace while they get me to where I need to be.

Twenty minutes later, we pull up outside the old building. I look at it as I climb out of the car, refastening my jacket.

"This is it? The building that you all want me to save?" I look to Elijah, who shrugs.

"I think it has character," he answers.

"It's a fucking dump that should have been knocked down thirty years ago," I reply, shaking my head in disbelief.

I look at the building again and feel my lip curl up in disgust. The stonework on the outside is a dull, dirty, dark grey; the windows are small and show no sign of life inside. Even the large clock on the roof of the building has long stopped working by the looks of it. Other than the electric door at the front, which shows lights on inside, I would think it was derelict.

"Let's get this shit done. I have a feeling I'll need a shower before my next meeting."

Vincent laughs as he casually leans against the car.

"You need me in there?"

I shake my head, turning to look at him.

"Unless you have the ability to fight off fleas, lice and ticks, I think I'll be okay." he continues to laugh as I walk up to the doors that open as I approach. I take a deep breath as I walk through them and into the library itself.

I look around at the internal walls, which are dull, and the paint is chipped in areas. The carpet is just as dull as everything else about the place. Even though there are no obvious signs of dirt, the place needs a freshen-up. The ceilings are high, and I have a feeling the upper floor is the same, judging from what I can see from where I'm standing.

"You've done what?"

A loud shout snaps me out of my trance as I look to the source of the disturbance.

Standing in the middle of the aisles is Councillor Frederick and a tiny woman with long brown silky hair that flows to the middle of her back in loose waves. She is standing in front of Fredrick as if she is plotting his demise. There's something about the way she's standing with her arms crossed over her chest, which makes blood rush to my cock.

Fuck, I bet she would make some adorable noises as she rode my dick, if it would fit in her, that is. She's so small I know I could have great fun corrupting and breaking her in.

I straighten my jacket as I head towards them. Fredrick warned me the librarian could be an issue, but I had imagined an old woman with a blue rinse. Not this tiny spitfire. The only problem I see I'm going to have is not bending her over that desk and fucking her in front of everyone.

Rose

"Isabelle, you need to understand that we have no more options here," Fredrick says, holding his hands up.

"I have an option for you: don't sell!" How the hell can he even consider selling this place? It's been part of the community for over a hundred years. Grandparents bring their grandkids here and share stories of their own childhood trips. My whole family has been coming here, right back to my grandmother being brought by her mother. You can't throw away history and tradition like that.

"Isabelle, you have to understand that funds have dried up; not enough people are coming through the doors to justify the council's continued funding."

"So, who's buying it? Are they keeping it as a library? Or are we going to find ourselves jobless?" I demand, placing my hands on my hips. Fredrick, the dick, lets out a sigh and rubs at his face.

"Look, a possible buyer will be here any minute. Just

show him around, let him get a feel for the place, and hopefully, he will keep it as it is."

My heart sinks as I realise there has been no confirmation of the new owner's plans for the place. I want to scream and shout, stomp my feet, and throw the biggest tantrum there is. I take a deep breath and cross my arms back over my chest as my jaw clenches.

"Who's coming to see it?" I ask through gritted teeth, hoping to at least attempt to keep my cool.

"I am."

I turn to the deep voice which came from behind me. I come face to face with a broad-suited chest. Looking up, I find greyish blue eyes looking at me with a broad grin underneath, flashing his pearly white teeth. For a moment, his eyes widen before his grin widens further.

"Adam Xander," he announces, offering his hand.

"I know who you are," I reply, refusing to take it as I turn to stare at Fredrick. Anger fills me like never before.

"Him! You are thinking of selling *to him*? Are you mad?"

Fredrick offers me a sad smile whilst shrugging.

"What exactly do you have against me? I wasn't aware we had met."

I turn to face him again, hoping he sees just how angry I am.

"We haven't," I snap. "But your reputation proceeds you, especially as you ruin every building you touch. If you don't turn it into one of your sleazy bars, you knock it down."

This man is a notorious billionaire playboy who thinks he can do whatever he wants. A day doesn't go by without him being in the papers or online. He's been dubbed by the press as Adam *"The Beast"* Xander because he's ruthless and cares about no one. He has no problem making an entire workforce jobless, and he's not doing that to me and my team.

"Well, I wouldn't call my bars sleazy, but the rest sounds about right."

I want to slap the smug look off that stupid face! What the hell is wrong with this man? How can he be so blasé about what he does? He truly has no consideration for other people.

"You are not getting your hands on this place! This is my library, my home, and if you think you are going to take it from me, you have another thing coming!"

That smirk on his face gets wider as he shoves his hands into his suit trouser pockets whilst rocking on the heels of his expensive, shiny shoes.

"And what is a tiny, feisty little thing like you going to do to stop me?"

I can hear the humour in his voice which just pisses me off even more.

"Just wait," I declare, taking a step forward, my hands on my hips. I refuse to let him intimidate me. "You will realise that you are messing with the wrong woman. You won't win this one, arsehole!" I spin on my heels and storm away, knowing full well if I stay there in front of him, I stand a real chance of being charged with murder. I can hear his deep laugh as I put as much distance between us as possible. If Councillor Fredrick thinks I'm going to show either of them around, he can think again.

"Isabelle, what's going on?"

I turn to see one of our regular visitors, Dorothy.

"The council is trying to sell the library to no other than Adam Xander!" I seethe through gritted teeth.

"Is he the good-looking one in the navy suit?" she asks, peeking around the side of the shelf. I roll my eyes at her.

"He's not that good-looking," I mutter, looking back at him. He's side on now, and as much as I hate to admit it, if I weren't furious with him, I probably would find him attractive. It's just a shame his attitude stinks. He is just some rich guy who was probably never told no as a child.

"I'm sorry to disagree with you, love, but that man is the definition of gorgeous, with a capital G! If I was thirty years younger, I certainly-"

"Wow, Dorothy, I don't need to know what you would do, and neither does anyone else here," I declare with my hands up.

I take a deep breath and look at the office where Aiden is working.

"I'll catch you in a bit. I need to go and calm down before I do something I might regret," I say as I walk past Dorothy and head for the office, needing to discuss this newest development with my friend.

I take a deep breath before entering and find him sitting at the desk surrounded by books that need cataloguing.

"Hey," Aiden turns in his chair, and his face drops when he sees me. "What's happened?"

I start talking at a million miles an hour as I explain the situation to Aiden, all whilst trying to stop myself from going back out there and kicking them out of the building. If Adam Xander thinks he's getting hold of my library, he can think again because others may not be able to tell him no, but I certainly can!

Precious Little Rose: Chapter Three

BEAST

"What do you want us to do today?" my architect asks as we stand outside the library.

"I want you to see if it is workable as a club or if we are going to need to knock the shithole down and build new on the grounds," I answer, straightening my tie. "But be warned, there is a lioness in there who is protective of her precious library and will give you a hard time."

Every time I think of the feisty woman with the long hazel hair having the balls to stand up to me, my cock twitches with the need to fill her. I now know her name is Isabelle Beaufort, and she likes to be referred to as Izzy. But I will never shorten her name as I rarely refer to her as Isabelle. To me, she is my Rose; she just doesn't know it yet.

My lips lift into a one-sided smirk as I remember the way her green eyes changed, the angrier she got, and how I could feel the anger radiating from her. It was a bigger turn-on than I have ever experienced, and it made me all the more desperate to get some alone time with her. No woman can resist a night with me; they may be weary at first, but eventually, they succumb to my charm, and if they don't, I will soon find someone else. But I'm not going to stop until I have this one. The need to corrupt and dominate that tiny body, ruining her for all other men, consumes me.

I stroll up to the doors, my shoulders pushed back and my most endearing smile. I turn to the reception desk, where the feisty Isabelle is talking on the phone. She looks up with a welcoming smile that perfectly shapes her red lips, but it slips the second she realises it's me.

"Get out! Right now!" she demands loudly whilst pointing to the doors.

"Now, Miss Beaufort, that's not very nice," I reply with a smile as I approach the counter. She quickly mutters something into the phone before hanging up and placing her hands on those hips that her yellow summer dress hugs perfectly.

"You're right it wasn't. Let me try again," she smirks. "Get the fuck out! Right now! Please." the sarcasm thrown into the last word makes me laugh out loud, which annoys her more. Her cheeks become flushed as her jaw clenches. She looks fucking adorable.

"The sale has gone through. There's nothing you can do to stop me from entering my own building," I point out as I put my hands in my pocket. The look on her face tells me the dickhead Fredrick hasn't told her like I asked him to. Fucking coward.

"What? It's only been a week!"

I don't miss the devastation on her face before it's replaced with a look of determination; I can't help but respect her. She stands to her full height; she may not be more than five feet, but she is ready to take down a whole damn army. My architect, Colin, clears his throat behind me, and I absent-mindedly wave for him to continue.

"Who the hell are you?" Isabelle demands as she storms from behind the desk and stands in front of him.

"Just a guy doing his job, miss," he says, holding his hands up. She crosses her arms over her chest, staring at him, and I can't blame Colin for taking a step back.

"How do you sleep at night knowing you work for that monster?"

Colin looks at me, but I just shrug and wave for him to leave. He rushes away, eager to escape Isabelle's line of fire. Luckily, she doesn't try to stop his helper as he follows after his boss, ducking away from the glare she throws his way while passing.

I chuckle, taking a step towards her, surprised by how much of a turn-on it is watching her belittling two grown-ass men. It's like this woman was made for me. When she turns her attention back to me, I swear my balls swell with my cock. Those green eyes burn a hole through my soul, and I know she sees depths of me that no other ever has. They have the same effect on me in the flesh as they did through the TV screen Saturday night.

"Has anyone ever told you how fucking hot you look when you're angry?" I ask with a smirk.

"No, they are too busy looking for their balls after I rip them off."

I burst out laughing at the little pit bull.

"This isn't over, Xander. I'll do everything I can to protect this library."

"I look forward to the challenge, Miss Beaufort," I reply, tipping an imaginary hat. She rolls her eyes before turning on her high heels and storming away from me. The tattoo on her shoulder catches my eye, and I find myself smiling further. Now that I've seen it in person, there is no mistaking that she is, in fact, the woman from the dance floor.

"A rose? Seems fitting."

"And what do you mean by that, Xander?" she yells, spinning to face me. I walk forward until I'm so close to her that she has to tip her head back to see me.

I look deep into those emerald gems she has for eyes as I answer.

"You are by far the most beautiful thing I have ever seen. Your tongue is as sharp as a thorn, which you use to keep people at arm's length. But like an eager bee, I want to see what happens if you let someone get close."

Isabelle takes a step forward, closing the distance between us. Like the vixen she is, she maintains eye contact the whole time.

"And you plan on getting close, do you?" she asks seductively.

"I plan on showing you how a real man fucks," I answer, straight to the point like always.

"Well, it's a shame I would rather fuck a dead horse than let you anywhere near my bed," she growls before turning and storming away.

"Then it's a good job I can think of a few other places then, little Rose," I call after her. She doesn't bother to reply; she just holds up her middle finger as she storms into the office at the side of the building. I laugh to myself whilst walking to where Colin and his guy are talking and taking measurements.

I look up at the tall ceiling and, for the first time, notice the beautiful paintwork. Looking around, I see the way the second floor circles above me, leaving a significant gap in the middle for the lower floor to see the ceiling. That's a massive health and safety issue. If I turn the place into a bar, I will have to change it so the second floor takes up the whole space, meaning the lower floor won't be able to see the artwork at all. I'm a little disappointed, as it seems a shame to hide it.

"You got your work cut out for you with that one, Xander," Colin calls, nodding towards the office door behind which Isabelle has disappeared.

"You have no idea; she'll make my life hell." I look around at the wall before us and place my hand against it. It's old but holds character. I had initially planned on this being a wine bar, but I think a gentlemen's club may be best.

"What's the chances of keeping the ceiling and having it refurbished?" I ask, pointing above me. Colin looks up, and I can see from his face that I won't like the answer.

"I'm not sure it will be worth the money. The artwork will be lost once you get your usual lighting in here. You might as well just remove it and paint it black, white, or red," he shrugs and looks back at me. But that's for your interior designer to work with. I just deal with the main structure."

I nod before looking back around.

"You know, keeping it as a library is always an option. That way, you could leave the building with character, it just needs a new lease of life."

I roll my eyes as I turn away from him, shaking my head.

"What is it about this place and everyone wanting to keep it as it is?" I sigh as I walk away. "Send me all the usual shit, and I will go through it all and get in touch," I call.

"Sure thing. I'll get it to you by tomorrow night."

"Tomorrow morning, Colin. I pay you enough to get the job done quickly," I reply as I walk past the office door and think of Isabelle inside, seething. Does the thought of me get her blood pumping like she does to me?

Fuck, I'm horny now.

The wank I had last night to the thought of her didn't take enough of the edge off. I need to fuck, and I need to do it soon.

I walk out into the cool air, retrieve my phone from my pocket, and pull up a number. I connect the call as Elijah holds the passenger door open for me.

"Office, please," I say as I wait for the call to connect. Elijah nods before closing the door and heading to the driver's seat.

"Adam, not heard from you for a while," her voice comes on the line.

"I've been busy. You free tonight?" I ask. Straight to the point, there's no need to pretend this is anything more than what it is—a way of release.

"I'm always free for you." I can hear the tease in her voice, but it's not a turn-on; if anything, it makes me consider hanging up the phone. Do I want a quick fuck when I could have a night with Isabelle Beaufort?

"I'll be at yours for eight," I reply, hanging up before she can answer. I place my phone beside me and grab the tablet I left on the seat.

"Piper?" Vinnie asks, smirking over his shoulder.

"Yeah, I need to let off some steam, and I can't be bothered looking for it," I reply, checking my emails on the tablet.

"It has nothing to do with a certain little brown-haired librarian, does it?" Eli chimes in as Vinnie laughs.

"Fuck off, the pair of you," I mutter, ignoring them laughing. I connect to another call whilst on the loudspeaker and wait for my second to answer.

"Xander, I thought you were at the library. Did Miss Beaufort kick you out of your own building?"

Vinnie and Elijah burst out laughing again as I tell them all to fuck off. I switch off the loudspeaker and lift the phone to my ear.

"You are all fucking hilarious," I growl under my breath as Thomas laughs. "If you have quite finished, I want all the background on Miss Beaufort and anyone else who works in the library." I bring the library website up on my tablet and check the employee page.

"How deep do you want me to go?" In other words, a standard search or one in which I learn their favourite food when they were three.

"Full works. I want to know if they are worth employing after I shut that place down." That's not a complete lie, but the main reason is I want to know everything about my little Rose.

"On it. Anything else?" Thomas asks.

"No, see you at four." I hang up and start looking through the information on the website in front of me. I don't know why I'm bothering I've already memorised everything on there about Isabelle.

Isabelle has worked in the library since the age of sixteen. Before then, she visited every weekend with her father. When she told me it was her home, she wasn't lying; everything in her life has revolved around that building and its damn books. I've already decided to give her a larger redundancy pay than everyone else who works there. I don't like the idea of her going short. I just haven't worked out when I will kick them all out yet.

Frederick put in the sale contract that I had to run the library for three months before I could turn it into anything else. I know there are ways around it, but I'm unsure if I want to close it yet.

When I walked into the library the other day to find the woman who had driven me mad with desire all weekend staring up at me, I thought all my Christmases had come at once. Not only had I found the woman I thought I never would, but she was within my grasp. I hadn't been sure if I would buy the property at that point, but as soon as I saw her there, my mind was set. If I had to use the library as a way in with her, I would.

I run my hand over my face as I look at her profile picture on my screen, her bright eyes sparkling as she smiles at the camera. It's the type of smile she had before she realised it was me in front of her. I want my little Rose to smile at me like that.

What the fuck has gotten into me? I don't give women nicknames or care whether they smile or not. I fuck and get out.

I turn off my tablet and throw it to the side of me, determined to think about anything other than that cock tease Isabelle Beaufort.

Precious Little Rose: Chapter Four

BEAST

"Oh! Yes!"

I'm balls deep in Piper, who's on her hands and knees in front of me as I pound into her hard and fast. I pull on her hair, giving her everything I have, but fuck it's not enough to get me off.

"Yes!" she cries out again. I growl through gritted teeth. Has she always been this vocal? I haven't noticed before, but tonight she's getting on my fucking nerves.

I look at her blonde hair wrapped around my hand and wonder what it would be like to have Isabelle's like this. The image jumps into my mind, and I groan as my cock hardens further. Closing my eyes, I imagine it's Isabelle in front of me, taking everything I give her as I pound her harder.

"Yes!" Piper calls out again, reminding me it's not the gutsy brunette I'm fucking.

"For fuck's sake," I growl, letting go of her hair and pulling out. I turn around and grab my trousers from where I left them.

"Is that it?" she asks from the bed as I pull off my condom.

"You wouldn't shut the fuck up," I snap, tying the empty rubber out of habit and pocketing it as I pull my trousers and pants up. Piper climbs off the bed and pulls on a dressing gown, tying it around her waist.

"You've never had a problem with the noises I make before," she sighs before walking forward and placing her hand on my bare chest. "Why don't you use my mouth instead? I'll have to stay quiet then," she suggests seductively. Taking her wrist, I remove her hand before taking a step back. I curse inwardly when I see the hurt in her eyes.

"No thanks." I quickly shrug on my shirt and pick up my shoes and jacket in the hope of getting out of here.

"So that's it, you're just going to fuck me and leave?"

I turn to face her, frowning.

"That's all this has ever been, Piper; you knew that from day one."

"Yeah, but I thought you enjoyed it. I thought-"

"You thought you could change my mind?" I sigh, pinching the bridge of my nose as I see the disappointment on her face. "I warned you this would always be sex and nothing else. I don't do relationships. You signed a contract knowing that." I try to ignore the way Piper starts sniffing, but I can't.

Fucking hell, why does she have to cry?

I turn to walk out and stop myself. "I'm sorry you got hurt. It wasn't my intention; I thought you knew the deal." I walk towards the door and stop again. "You deserve better than someone like me," I add before leaving her place as quickly as possible, not wanting to make her feel worse than she already does.

I climb into my car and sit behind the wheel.

Why do they always have to develop feelings? Why can't women just fuck, and that's it?

Because they are not heartless bastards like you. That tedious voice in my head taunts. Well, It's not wrong.

I have never dated; if I did, it was only for convenience, not because I liked a woman. I've never developed feelings for any of them until Isabelle.

I reach for my phone and check my emails. There's one from Thomas, which I open eagerly.

Inside is Isabelle's file, as I had hoped. I open the attachment and start to read through it. There isn't much I didn't already know. I pull up her address and type it into the Satnav to check out where she lives. I realise I'm only fifteen minutes away and head off, planning to check out the area.

I rarely get to drive myself, so tonight, I'm going to make the most of it. I put some music on and relax whilst driving through the quiet town. Leaning my arm out the open window, I drive one-handed, enjoying the peace and quiet of not having anyone around.

Vinnie insists on being with me most of the time, which is probably wise as I didn't earn the title *"The Beast"* by sitting behind a desk. I don't take no for an answer, and I'm happy to get violent to get what I want.

My hands have been dirty since I took my first life at nineteen years of age. That bastard deserved to die, and my only regret is that I didn't know the torture techniques I do now. He should have suffered rather than a quick bullet to the head.

I run my fingers through my hair and take a deep breath as my hand tightens around the wheel. I refuse to waste any more time thinking of that prick. Instead, I let out my breath and think about the woman whose house

I'm heading towards—the beautifully feisty Isabelle Beaufort.

I pull into her street and slowly check out the area. The buildings are old, and I bet many structural issues exist. The houses are all semi-detached, with front gardens and small driveways, which lead to what I'm guessing are small back gardens. The buildings aren't big, maybe two or three bedrooms, but I can't imagine the mortgage or rent is cheap on them. How does she manage with the minimal wage she brings home from the library? Does she have a second job? Or does she have a housemate to help share the bills?

I spot her house number and come to a stop outside, parking on the other side of the road. I look at her home and smile when I spot two rose bushes, one on either side of her front window. A Ford Focus is parked in the driveway, and a car is outside her house. I grab my phone and pull up Vinnie's number.

"That was quick," he teases as he answers.

"Don't fucking start; I left there as quickly as possible. She got needy," I sigh, not wanting to admit the truth. I didn't want to be fucking anyone but my little Rose.

"Damn, time to find a new one, then. What's up?"

"I need you to check a registration for me." I wait for him to grab a pen and paper and then read off the licence plates of the cars outside of Isabelle's house. Vinnie tells me he will call me back and hangs up. I close the window to ensure she won't see me if she looks out into the street and open the file I now have saved on my phone.

It says here she has lived in this house her whole life. I skim through the family history; her mother died when she was very young. Her father is still alive, and there is no mention of siblings, spouses, or children. That's one less thing to worry about, I don't sleep with other people's wives, and I plan fucking her very soon. There is mention of a couple of exes; I don't recognise their names, so I push it to the back of my mind. Exes don't matter unless they are causing an issue.

My phone rings, and I answer it quickly.

"Where are you?" Vinnie asks suspiciously.

"None of your business," I reply, rolling my eyes.

"I'm your head of security; you pay me to make it my business."

"Have you got something for me or not?" I sigh.

"Yeah, the first one belongs to Isabelle Beaufort, but I think you knew that since you are sitting outside her house like a crazy ass stalker."

"Vincent," I growl in warning as he laughs. "The second one?"

"Belongs to Aiden Class."

That guy who works in the library? Are they together? I look to the house and can almost see the two of them fucking as I sit out here, horny and alone.

"Before you go all Hulk, he's gay," I hear Vinnie laugh down the phone.

"How gay?" I demand through gritted teeth.

"Never had a girlfriend, lived with a guy until two weeks ago, gay."

I relax a little, but I still feel uneasy about my girl being in a house with another guy.

Fuck, what's with this, *my girl* and nickname shit? Didn't I *just* tell Piper I don't date?

"I'll be home in a bit," I tell Vinnie before hanging up.

I look back to the house and check for CCTV cameras or any other security, but I see nothing. I can see that most houses on the street have cameras outside, so why doesn't she? That needs to change. I make a note to check the crime rate in the local area, just to be on the safe side. She needs to be protected.

I open her employment file on my phone and get her email before sending her a message. I need to put this whole obsession to rest and move the hell on before I lose my motherfucking mind over this woman.

Precious Little Rose: Chapter Five

ROSE

Climbing out of my car, I look around the empty car park, expecting someone to be there watching me. There isn't another vehicle in sight, and the roads are quiet, yet I still feel uneasy in my gut.

I've been on edge for the last few weeks for no reason at all. I'm sure it's nothing, but I can't shake it. Aiden thinks it's to do with the library being sold and that I've been stressed. But I don't think I have ever felt this way before, especially here of all places. Whatever is causing it needs to stop, as I don't have time for it.

I unlock the doors to the main entrance before rushing inside to turn off the alarm. Placing my bag on the reception desk, I return to the doors to relock them. The last thing I want is for someone to walk in whilst I'm so jumpy. I need at least one more cup of coffee before I tackle all that I need to do this morning, which includes replying to a certain arsehole's email.

I drag out making my coffee as much as possible, not

eager to start up the computer as it will mean acknowledging said mail. But eventually, when Aiden arrives an hour later, I have no choice but to face the music.

Miss Beaufort.
I believe we have gotten off on the wrong foot, and I would like to put this right.
I will be at the library at 14:00 tomorrow to discuss a few things. Please ensure you are available at this time.
I look forward to getting a chance to speak to you.
Sincerely
A. Xander

"So, are you going to talk to him?" Aiden asks over my shoulder. I shrug, take a deep breath and sit back in my chair.

"Like I said last night, I don't think there is anything left to say. He seems pretty set on destroying this place. I don't know if anything I could do would make a difference at this point."

Aiden places a hand on my shoulder and squeezes it slightly before kissing my cheek.

"It couldn't hurt to try. You got this, Izzy."

He walks away as I look around at the library. I don't want to give up on this place; it is too important to me, but I don't know what to do anymore.

Aiden and I sat up late into the night, trying to devise ideas for the best way to show Adam how important this library is to people. The only things we have come up with are a protest and a petition, but I'm unsure if any of that would help. I guess it's worth a try; what more have I got to lose?

Grab your copy…

vinci-books.com/preciouslittlerose

About the Author

D.E. Bartley lives in Wales, UK, with her husband, three feral boys, four cats, and a budgie.

To say her home is a madhouse would be an understatement, but she wouldn't have it any other way.

When she isn't running around after her tribe or driving her husband up the wall, she can be found reading and hoarding books like a dragon.

Nothing is as important to her as time with her family, and she loves her trips home to Cornwall with them more than anything in the world. What could possibly compare to sitting on a Cornish beach, with a glass of Cornish gin in one hand and an authentic Cornish pasty in the other, while the monsters, I mean children, play and bodyboard in the sea?

Absolutely nothing.

Acknowledgments

I very nearly never wrote this book. I was going to leave *Ladling with Luke* as a stand-alone and forget about it. But there was something about Lily and Dan's story that kept pulling me back until I could think of nothing else, and I knew I had to write it for them. Now I'm so glad I did, as I love the chemistry between them and how they tried to hide and fight their growing love for one another.

Thank you to my friends who persuaded me I would regret not following my heart and putting this story out there; as it turns out, you are right, every character deserves their own HEA.

Most importantly, thank you to each of my readers who begged for this story and couldn't wait to get their hands on it. Your support means so much to me. Thank you from the bottom of my heart.

www.ingramcontent.com/pod-product-compliance
Lightning Source LLC
LaVergne TN
LVHW041108190826
845923LV00037B/617

* 9 7 8 1 0 3 6 7 3 3 8 6 5 *